Girl Lost at Sea

An Ella Porter Mystery Thriller

Georgia Wagner

Contents

to actual persons, living or dead, and events or locations is entirely coincidental.

Chapter 1

The young woman shivered near the crab pots, standing on the slick, metal deck, a gloved hand gripping the frigid railing as sea spray speckled her face.

She shivered, her teeth chattering, her hood raised as another breaker wave splashed against the brow of *Queen's Gambit*—the king crabbing vessel.

Caitlin Grimberg was new to the vessel. A greenhorn. And as such, it had been her job to tie the first row of crab pots. Three ties per pot. One to secure on either side; one to secure to the pots beneath.

Now, she stood on the edge of the deck as the other crab fishermen moved about her. At only seventeen-years-of-age, Caitlin was the youngest person on the *Queen's Gambit* by far. A few of the rougher sailors would occasionally shoot glances at her that made her uncomfortable or offer snide remarks that she preferred to ignore.

But no one was overt in their ogling or commentary. Her father was the captain of the crabbing vessel, after all.

It had been *his* idea to get her this job. Always daddy's girl, she'd never balked at a challenge. Not when he'd signed her up for ice hockey nor when he'd placed her in advanced courses. And now...

She was determined to see this through as well.

She stood on the deck as another wave hit the prow. Water splashed over the railing, slick on the floor. Men in rain slickers and thick boots were wrangling one of the crab pots, dumping the large, twenty-pound crabs into the holding compartment.

She watched as a crew member named Donavan swung a grappling hook over his head then launched it out into the sea. Even as another wave rocked the boat, the hook snared the trailing, red buoy marking where they'd left their row of crab pots.

The tall stack of large cages, nearly twice the size of a golden retriever's kennel, tottered above her. She winced, staring, desperately counting the ties in her head.

She didn't want to have to climb that twenty-foot pile of metal mesh again. She'd seen men break their arms managing the things. She'd heard of even worse.

Now, as she stared up at the towering wall of metal pots, she felt a flicker of relief as the ties she'd secured kept them steady. No collapsing tower this trip.

At least there was that comfort.

"Hang on, Caitie!" called a voice behind her.

She turned, holding a hand up to shield her eyes from the saline spray as a man with a white beard stumbled past her. His hand tapped her shoulder, roughly pushing her to the side as he hastened to help the crew pull the next crab pot up.

Her father had never been gentle with her. But she watched, impressed as the seasoned captain maneuvered over the slick deck in the middle of the rolling Bering Sea with practiced ease, as if he were striding confidently across a dance floor.

He reached the edge of the rail, flung out a large hand, and snared the edge of the pot as they pulled it, hoisting it to the deck with the rope from the hook the deckhand had thrown.

The red buoy was pulled free, tossed to the side where the trailing rope couldn't tangle any legs.

And then the men began to heave the pot.

"Heavy one!" someone was shouting. "Gotta be at our limit now!"

"Might be going home early boys, hoist away!" shouted her father. "Come on! Put some grease into it!"

She watched, impressed as their muscles strained, and the men worked together to wrangle the pot onto the deck.

She hesitated as they did, though, staring faintly, frowning. Crabs were spilling out of this pot. Strange, large, alien creatures with giant claws and armored shells. She couldn't hear them scuttling or clicking over the sound of the rolling seas, but she watched the way their tiny, elongated eyestalks shifted back and forth as they clambered over each other, trying to avoid the grasping hands of the crabbers as the prey were measured against measuring implements, determining if they were a permitted catch.

Now, she glanced back over the opposite railing, looking away.

She hadn't told her father—she couldn't imagine how that conversation might go—but she often felt sympathy for the crabs, as creepy and scary as they looked.

As she looked away, not wanting to watch the capture of a new host of crabs, she peered into the sea.

Briefly, as the waves rolled away and the ship continued its circuit, following the chain of pots and red buoys they'd placed earlier in the season, the water seemed to still.

The waves were still rolling a hundred paces behind them, but here, a brief lull had fallen. She stared into the water, her brow furrowed, her eyes straining despite the sting of the salty spray.

There, below her, she spotted something.

Two red buoys, tangled up in a line.

And attached to the buoys, far, far too *close* to the surface, was a crabbing pot. A rusted metal cage, floating on the water thanks to the buoys.

"What's that?" she said, not loud enough for anyone to hear. "Dad?" she called out over her shoulder, frowning as she turned back to peer into the water.

She stared, certain she was seeing things.

Then, she heard yelling. "Caitie! Caitie, get away from the rail. It's a breaker! Caitie!"

She began to turn, but too slowly.

In her distraction, leaning forward, she hadn't spotted the wave approaching from the *opposite* side of the ship. Starboard, aft, port—the names she knew she was supposed to memorize but had never quite managed to.

Now, as she whirled around, a giant geyser of water struck the vessel from the opposite side, slamming into the metal hull of the *Queen's Gambit*.

She briefly glimpsed the horrified look on her father's bearded face, watched as he lunged for her even though he was a good ten paces away. He practically football tackled through the air, trying to reach her.

And then the whole ship twisted on its side. It wouldn't sink. But the momentum of the wave sent her stumbling back...

Into the metal rail, which struck her spine.

Then over the rail.

She screamed as she fell. Tumbling backward into the sea.

The boat was traveling so fast.

She'd been warned. The one thing she'd been warned.

Do not fall into the water. Whatever happens... Don't fall into the water.

And now, she plummeted into the murk with a calamitous splash! Water in her eyes, her lungs. She desperately tried to spit the liquid free but to no avail. She was now swallowing a mountain of liquid. Salt in her eyes, her mouth, her nostrils. The murk suspended her, holding her fast in its swaying, undulating motion.

She kicked, and her legs were weighty. Her instantly soaked clothing was now an encumbrance.

What was it her father had said?

Follow the trail of bubbles.

Right... the bubbles streaming past her face... She had to follow the bubbles, didn't she? As long as no flush of current redirected them.

And so she breathed a small amount, loosing the bubbles. They chu rned... past her cheek, up, up... That was up!

Desperation fueled her. She kicked, trying to rise. The reason she'd been wearing the stupid, bright orange jacket with the reflective pieces had been at her mother's insistence.

And now, she hoped they'd be enough for the crew to spot her in the water.

She kicked up, her head bursting from the murk. Water was still rising around her, rolling like constantly moving hills.

Caitlin felt the deep, dark waters clenching around her body, threatening to carry her away. She could barely see anything in the pitch blackness that surrounded her, only faintly lit shapes of strange and unfathomable depths. Every time she tried to move forward, the grasping arms of the sea seemed to hold her back.

Every time she attempted to swim, she felt her limbs turn to lead, each effort becoming harder and more futile. She was completely exhausted from the sheer effort of maintaining her head above water. Liquid in her mouth, her ears, her eyes. She spat, desperately, her eyes stinging, her nostrils too. She could feel the strain of the water... So little time, yet so much energy. She had been in school only last week... And now? Near the point of giving up. She was so far from the distant boat—which was still churning away, but slowly—so very, very slowly—turning.

She held onto the last shred of hope that she might be able to stay afloat but feared that it was a fool's errand. Her muscles ached and her lungs burned. She was so bone-tired that she thought she might sink beneath the surface at any moment. She'd already worked a double shift on the crabbing vessel.

She'd already been exhausted.

And now this?

It seemed like the sea itself was alive, a sinister force that was determined to keep her from her father's vessel. She could feel its grip on her, pulling her down and threatening to crush the life out of her. She had no idea how far she had come, how much farther she had to go, or if succeeding was even a possibility.

But despite the darkness, she kept on trying to swim forward, towards the boat, her mind focused on the distant *Queen's Gambit*. She could just make out the silhouette of it in the darkness, a beacon of hope that kept her going. It was still turning and now looked as if it were crashing back towards her, against the waves. She refused to give into despair, refused to believe that she was doomed. Refused to accept that this was her final resting place.

She kept pressing forward, her strokes becoming weaker and weaker as fatigue set in. She was so close, yet so far, the boat seeming to get further away with each passing moment. She began to feel hopelessness settle over her, the all-encompassing darkness beginning to close in.

And then, out of nowhere, she felt a hand grab her wrist. She gasped in terror and then felt a gentle tug. She was being pulled. Someone was helping her.

But how was that possible?

The boat was still so, so far away.

She blinked dark droplets of liquid from her eyes, trying to wave a hand to clear her features. She managed a desperate breath, spitting droplets and staring through the dark.

Two, bright orange buoys caught her attention.

She stared, frozen in place, bobbing in the water, staring at the hand gripping her wrist.

Except it wasn't quite *gripping* her. More like it had snagged on her sleeve.

And the hand...

The hand was made of bone. Spindly, skeletal fingers, nipped clean by crabs and underwater creatures. The crabbing cage, upheld by the two orange buoys, bobbed at her side.

She stared into it, gaping at the leering skeletal face staring back at her.

She would've screamed again if she had the energy.

But now, all she could do was gasp, hold onto the crabbing pot for dear life, avoid the hand jutting through the metal. A hand extending towards her as if searching for aid in an unending cry for help.

She spotted a second skeleton curled in the shadows of the water, the storm-tossed current sloshing over the two skeletons trapped in the cage. The one with its arm extended towards her was rigid, frozen in that posture.

The other had its arms wrapped around the first.

The two skeletons were snared in some infinite embrace, floating on the water, sloshing about, the two buoys holding them aloft.

And only then, did Caitlin manage to summon the strength to scream.

A bright light shone towards her, suddenly. The search light from the boat—a composite of two flashlights, brighter than the high-beams of most trucks.

The bright light found the buoys, found her flashing jacket.

"Caitlin!" a desperate voice yelled. "Hang on!"

She did, gripping the rusted cage tight but unable to look away. Unable to look towards the vessel careening in behind her, coming to rescue her.

Far from the shores of Nome, Alaska, where her father's vessel sailed from, all she could stare at, as salt dappled her lips, as the water thrashed at her skin, as the chill nip of the sea settled in her own bones...

All she could *see* were the two embracing skeletons, trapped in a crabbing cage, far, far, far out at sea.

Chapter 2

Ella Porter nodded politely over the table between them, flashing a faint smile which didn't quite reach her eyes.

Supervising Agent Hamlin sat across the table from her. The woman had a short buzz cut and the gaunt face of someone who'd battled more than chemo in her days but had come back strong. Now the woman with the close-cut hair and business suit had leaned across the table, checking the recording device between them.

"So you don't know Mr. Graves?" Agent Hamlin asked, glancing up again.

The woman wore makeup in tasteful quantities. Her skin was bronze, though her haggard expression suggested that the foundation concealed a natural pallor. The woman frowned as she said, "It was suggested by some of the locals that you were familiar with the man."

Ella gave a faint, polite shake of her head then lied through her teeth. "He was there when we arrived," she said. "I believe I met him, but he claimed to be a tourist."

The lie tumbled so easily from her lips, she felt a bout of shame. Her friend, Brenner Gunn, often said she had a knack for lying. But he accused her of lying not so much with her words as with her politeness. Her pleasant disposition.

Ella strongly believed that one could catch more flies with honey.

Brenner strongly believed that flies were best stomped underfoot.

The two of them had been an unlikely pairing over the last couple of weeks...

Now, though, Ella had sat through her *third* round of interviews concerning the experiences with the Spring Children, a cult in the wilderness who'd been sacrificing young women as part of their grisly rituals.

"Well..." said Agent Hamlin slowly, "At least this business was settled. Though next time..." she eyed Ella. "It would be appropriate to check-in with Seattle before galivanting off."

Ella nodded demurely. "Of course, ma'am. Apologies."

Hamlin sighed, closing her eyes for a moment and rubbing the bridge of her nose.

"Are we done?" Ella asked, keeping her tone even.

The agent paused, studying Ella briefly. She leaned back in her chair now and eyed the younger woman. "You're twenty-eight?" she said.

Ella blinked at the presumption.

"I…" she didn't know what to say.

But the agent just shrugged. Hamlin sighed. "I remember being your age… What I don't remember," she said slowly, as she sat in the metal chair across the desk, under a window that overlooked the blue seas under equally blue skies, "is why someone like you… with your track record… was sent to this podunk town."

Ella flickered. "I grew up here," she said reflexively. "My family operates gold mines."

The agent looked impressed. "Huh. Well… I guess that makes sense." The woman glanced back to the folder resting on the smooth, metal table between them. She didn't open the folder, and Ella had the impression, up to this point, that Agent Hamlin had already *memorized* everything in the file. The only reason she glanced down at it was out of some pretend humility, hoping to keep Ella at ease.

But without looking up, nor opening the folder, Hamlin said, "Your case closure rate was impressive. I've been over some of your files. Someone might say you were a rising star." She smiled now and looked up. "What's your secret, Agent Porter?"

Ella blinked, taken off guard.

Hamlin was clearly a shrewd operator. But Ella also didn't want to be *too* cynical. Perhaps the older woman was just being polite.

In a way, the two of them were still feeling each other out. Were still measuring the other.

Hamlin was cleaning up all the red tape from the Spring Children arrests. Centuries-old murders had taken place... All of them solved thanks to Ella and Brenner... And their unlikely ally in Mortimer Graves.

Also known as the Graveyard Killer. This small, but crucially important fact, wasn't known to *anyone* else.

Certainly not Agent Hamlin.

Ella just shrugged politely. She said, "I don't know what to tell you. I guess I was lucky."

The woman across the table smiled. "Humble, too, I see."

Ella just shrugged again. If she had to be *honest* about it... she had her guesses regarding her success with the bureau. Ella's attention to detail and her memory were two of the biggest factors in her case closures... Not the *biggest* factor. No. The *main* reason she'd succeeded as an agent had to do with a part of her most never saw.

She didn't let them. And with good reason.

A will of iron in a small, pretty woman was often accused of being something more malicious.

No... no, she preferred playing cheerleader.

But when she approached a case? The pretend was discarded.

Stubborn with a smile, that's how she saw herself.

Now, Ella repeated her question from earlier, her tone still light and cautious. "So... are we done?" Her eyes darted to the recorder on the table, illuminated in the thin strand of sunlight coming through the open window above Agent Hamlin.

The agent blinked a few times as if staving off sleep, then sighed, clicking off the recording device and making a shooing motion towards the door. "No. I'll still have some more questions. But for now..." She shrugged.

Ella felt a surge of relief as she regained her feet, gave a farewell nod, and then hurried towards the door, smoothing the front of her own neat, second-hand business suit which she had ironed twice this morning in anticipation of the meeting.

Appearances mattered, in Ella's opinion.

And her own appearance was one that often had been likened to a cheerleader a few years past her prime. At twenty-eight-years-old, Ella was hardly *old*. In fact, to most, she was the greenhorn at the agency.

To many, thanks to her impressive case closure rate and her two master's degrees in Criminal Psychology and Behavioral Science, she'd been a rising star.

Until she'd let a notorious serial killer escape.

The Graveyard Killer.

What no one knew was that she'd let him go free on purpose.

And no one would *ever* know. If they found out?

It was over for her.

She closed the door slowly behind her as her smile slipped. Appearances certainly mattered, and Ella often attended to hers.

She had pure blonde hair, like spun gold; pale blue eyes like frozen seas; and a pretty, upturned celestial nose.

Her clothing, though neat, was second-hand. She always purchased her clothing second-hand. She simply didn't see the point in spending the money. Ella didn't own a car, and she rented the cheapest unit she could find back in her hometown of Nome, Alaska, and it was something of a matter of pride how frugally she lived.

Unlike her family.

Sometimes, she wondered if her aversion to her family's lifestyle wasn't nearly the guiding compass she wanted it to be.

But now...

She shook her head, pushing through the small sheriff's station they'd been permitted to use. She glanced through the glass, spotting where Brenner Gunn's truck waited in the parking lot.

She felt a flash of gratitude that he'd waited for her.

She didn't look back. Didn't scan the small police station for her brother-in-law, Chief Baker. Certainly didn't look for her sister Priscilla, who was...

But then, Ella paused as she pushed through the door of the station.

A cold breeze wafted through, and she shivered. There, leaning against the hood of Brenner's truck, her sister Priscilla was chatting animatedly.

Priscilla was smiling happily and enjoying the look of extreme discomfort on Brenner Gunn's features.

Ella wiped the frown from her face as she approached, watching the two of them warily.

"Oh, come on, Brenner," Priscilla was saying conversationally. She had the same features as her twin sister. But besides their looks, Priscilla with her upturned nose and pretty features topped by golden hair, the two sisters couldn't have been more different.

Priscilla was wearing her favorite seashell earrings.

Just another dig at Ella.

Ella had been deathly scared of the ocean and the deep water since she'd been sixteen—an incident that had left her scarred. As if wanting to constantly *remind* Ella, Priscilla seemed to wear the earrings from the sea as a sort of taunt.

Now, Priscilla was laughing and reaching through the window to pat Brenner on the arm. "You really do know how to pick 'em, Brenner," Priscilla was saying conversationally, speaking loud enough so Ella could hear, though, she hadn't acknowledged her sister's approach yet.

Brenner Gunn, on the other hand, the only US Marshal in town, just stared determinedly ahead, ignoring Cilla.

"Come on, you used to be so fun," Priscilla was saying, trailing her finger along Brenner's arm clad in flannel.

Brenner again didn't reply, just staring through the windshield, his eyes fixated on the glass, his jaw set and rigid.

As she approached, Ella felt her temper flaring. She didn't *lose* her temper. In fact, she couldn't quite remember the last time she'd *truly* lost it. She simply channeled her anger in... *other* ways.

Sky-diving, piloting lessons, spelunking, para-gliding in Panama... just a few of the activities that helped her blow off steam. The sorts of activities most of her friends and family didn't know about. A peek behind the curtain that was Eleanor Porter.

But now, as she reached the side of the truck, her feet tapping against the cold asphalt outside the sheriff's office, she shot a quick glance towards Brenner, studying his silhouette.

Brenner Gunn had been the only good thing about returning to Nome.

She'd managed to get out of the sheltered hometown. But he... he was stuck, in a way. He'd managed a couple of tours, overseas, had even served as a sniper for the SEALs. An elite marksman. But then he'd injured his right leg—and he still walked with a limp to this day.

But the sight of him? Even from here... certainly wasn't a bad one.

They'd been childhood sweethearts in their teens, but Brenner—also twenty-eight—had gotten even prettier with age. Those blue eyes, that chiseled jaw. A single burn mark, though, traced under the side of his chin, up to his left ear. He scratched at it, absentmindedly, studying her with his solemn, clear-sky gaze.

A few inches over six-foot, apparent even as he sat in the front seat of his truck, Brenner Gunn really was the handsomest man she'd ever met.

Handsome... pretty... but also sad.

Pretty and sad.

She wasn't sure if he would've liked this characterization.

Ella Porter, stubborn with a smile. Brenner Gunn, pretty and sad.

She smiled, forcing it across her lips. Inwardly, she thought, *stop tormenting him, you jerk.* But like always, Ella paused, reconsidered her speech, and chose a less incendiary approach.

"Hello, Cilla," she said conversationally, forcing some good cheer into her voice.

Her sister turned, looking at Ella. She didn't smile, didn't blink. Instead, she scratched at one of her seashell earrings. "Huh," Cilla said. "Something smells, Brenner. Check your boots."

"Just get out of here, will you?" Brenner said, exhausted, as if knowing full well this request wouldn't matter in the least to Cilla.

Priscilla Porter *did as she wanted.* She always had.

21

Where the Porter family gold dynasty had intended to create princesses... it hadn't stuck with Ella. But Priscilla had taken to the position—now helping to run the family's inland mining operations—like a duck to water.

A very annoying duck who quacked a lot.

"Oh, don't get your panties in a bunch, Brens," Cilla said, patting Brenner on the arm. Then, with a smirk, she strode past Ella as if she wasn't even there.

Ella and Brenner both watched as Cilla approached the door to her husband's office—Chief Baker had once been a football star in Nome, so it had been a fitting match between Priscilla and the king of the cops.

Ella sighed as her sister left, feeling a slow relief.

But before Priscilla had stepped through the door of the station, the woman paused, glanced back, smirked and said, "I hear you're having some trouble with the feds."

Ella didn't frown. She liked to think she had a pretty good poker face. But she did feel her stomach twist.

"Oh?" Ella said, tilting an eyebrow.

"Mhmm... My interview with Agent Hamlin is this afternoon, in fact," Priscilla said, beaming. "I can't wait for our chat. She wants to know *all* about you, Eleanor."

And then, certainly aware of the unease her words had left, Priscilla turned on her heel, bobbed her head in a nod a single time, as if she'd finally accomplished what she'd intended, and disappeared back into the precinct.

Ella and Brenner both frowned after her.

Once she'd gone, Brenner cleared his throat. "Shit... She sure as hell doesn't like you."

Ella sighed. "She seems to like you a lot."

Brenner snorted, shaking his head, and glancing over his flannel-sleeved shoulder at her. "Nah. She just knows that coy bullshit pisses me off. Say, I got you a ride, but you might needa cancel any plans."

Ella moved around the side of the truck, frowning, but holding her question until she slipped into the cabin. "Sorry—cancel plans?" she said.

"Mhmm. Something came up."

He started the engine, adjusting his baseball cap which he so often wore over those pretty, sky-blue eyes.

"What?" she said, hesitant. "Not... not with Hamlin?"

"Nah. Already had my interview. She kept asking about that creepy friend of yours."

"Oh?" Ella said, hesitantly.

Brenner didn't know who Mortimer Graves was either. Not in the least. She wondered if he'd turn her in then and there if she told him. So instead, she kept her face expressionless.

But Brenner replied, "Yeah... I didn't say shit. Just some tipster, right? Your old CI?"

"Yeah... yes, certainly."

It didn't feel good to lie to Brenner. But it would've felt far, far worse for him to find out the truth about the Graveyard Killer.

Besides, Mortimer Graves had left Nome. She hadn't heard from him in days.

Just the way she liked it.

For now, under wide open skies and with the seas ahead, as they moved through the small town of Nome, it felt as if she had a new lease on life.

Her hometown wasn't *that* bad. Especially with the interview with Hamlin no longer hanging over her head.

As they traversed the streets in Brenner's truck, Ella glanced out the window.

Nome, Alaska was a small city of about 3,500 people located on the western coast of the state, a little over 300 miles from Anchorage. This city was considered to be the most remote incorporated city in the United States, and as such, was home to some of the most unique streets and architectural styles in the country.

As their truck pulled up the roads, Ella noted the rugged, yet charming mix of old and new structures that lined the streets, including buildings from the early nineteen-hundreds when Nome was first established as a mining town, as well as modern structures and business developments. This mix of old and new gave Nome a unique charm that set it apart from other cities in Alaska.

The streets of Nome were lined with brightly colored buildings, ranging from bright reds to deep blues. The streets of Nome also featured some of the most picturesque views of the Bering Sea and snow-capped mountains in the distance.

Ella smiled as she gazed at the distant mountains and the way they stood like sentries against the sky.

But her momentary cheer was short-lived as Brenner said, "Got a case for you."

"You do?"

"Mhmm."

"How come it's coming through the Marshals?"

"Cuz," Brenner said. "Victim was an escaped convict." He gave her a significant look, tugging at the brim of his hat.

She sighed, massaging her temples. "Okay... Alright. When—er, *where*?"

"Taking us there now," he said. "Needa stop for coffee?"

"Where is it, Brenner?"

He winced, shooting her a quick look. "You don't... still have that thing about big bodies of water, do you?"

She stared at him, her face a mask.

He snorted, looking away. "You're lying again," he said.

"I didn't say anything!"

"Exactly," he muttered. "Lie of omission."

She frowned. "Maybe I don't think it appropriate to share *every* emotion that crosses my mind with you. Ever think of that?"

But Brenner shook his head. "I know you, Ella."

"So this is on the sea, is it? Where? A lighthouse?"

"Crabbing boat," he said. "They brought the victims back to shore. Still there, actually."

"Not with the coroner?" she said, trying to suppress the rising sense of unease. She hated the idea that she'd have to face the water. But if the victims were brought to *shore,* perhaps she'd only have to face her hated nemesis of the seas around Nome from a distance.

But Brenner said, "Coroner is gonna meet us there. Two victims were identified by an ID on the fugitive. Nothing else is left."

"What do you mean?"

Brenner shot her another look. "Picked clean," he said simply. "Skeletons. They were found in a crabbing cage."

"A... a cage? Like an underwater cage?"

He nodded once, and she felt a faint shiver.

She turned to stare back through the windshield as Brenner drove them to the crime scene.

Now, somehow, the sky didn't seem so blue. The sun didn't seem so bright. Two bodies found trapped in a cage at the bottom of the sea...

It was the fuel of nightmares.

She grimaced and rubbed her hands slowly together, wondering what *new* horror the Bering Sea had washed ashore this time.

Chapter 3

Ella moved forward, carefully, stepping over the metal barrier separating the parking lot from the sandy shore by the dock where the crabbing vessels launched.

Gulls flew overhead, cawing. The seabirds swooped like gray and white kites under the sun as the bright swathe of blue water sparkled.

The allure of the ocean was somewhat lost on her.

She moved down an incline, towards where the cage settled. A couple of cops had been stationed to keep dockworkers from the cage which had been left on the shore per the local precinct's request.

And the coroner, by the look of things, hadn't shown up yet.

Brenner's truck door slammed as he followed behind, throwing a long leg over the metal barrier and coming after her.

Ella swallowed her trepidation, her feet carrying her forward, closer to the crabbing pot. In the fading light of the sun, it seemed to be calling out to her. She could feel the rising tension, an unseen force pressing down on her shoulders.

The sand beneath her feet was still damp from the waves that had come and gone, leaving behind a residue of tiny shells and stones. A salty scent filled her nose and a gentle breeze cooled her skin. She reached the pot, the two skeletons visible in the soft light. There was something strange about them. Not only were the bones different, but they seemed to be arranged in a certain way.

Ella knelt down and began to examine the bones. She could tell that the ribs of one skeleton were elongated and the other was slightly narrower. It was as if one of them had been in the pot longer than the other. She carefully touched each bone, her nose inches away from them. The sensation of the cold, hard remains of someone's life was strange and eerie.

Ella felt a chill run through her body, her heart beating so fast it almost felt like it was trying to escape her chest. She closed her eyes and tried to focus, but the energy of the moment was too powerful to ignore. She opened them again to find the skeletons looking right at her.

In the fading light of the sun, Ella wondered what could have happened to these two people. What had brought them to this beach, so far away from home? Who were they? What had they been searching for in the depths of the sea?

Ella had no answers, only questions that she suspected would remain unanswered. After a few moments, she stood up and brushed the sand off her knees.

She made a mental note to ask the coroner about the ribs when the woman arrived.

For now, she heard the crunch of shells and sand as Brenner approached, his shadow stretching over the ground as he drew near her.

She glanced through the bars of the cage. "They just left this here?"

Brenner grunted. He stood near her, and his breath plumed over her shoulder, a small jet of mist on the air. "My office was contacted first while I waited for you in the parking lot. I just told them to leave it where no one could tamper with it."

She glanced towards two police officers who she recognized from the Nome department. Both of them worked under Baker. And both of them, as she examined their faces, looked vaguely familiar. Football players from back in the day, she realized as her memory slotted them into place. She didn't need a yearbook to remember them.

One of the benefits she'd always had was her memory.

Now, she gestured at one of the officers, who looked bored, standing near one of the wooden posts supporting the large dock.

On the other side of the structure, a crabbing vessel was being roped off to mooring posts lining a cement barricade.

Another vessel, further down, had been lashed to the dock already. And Ella watched as sailors disembarked, or lingered on the dock, smoking cigarettes.

She could gauge by the expressions on the sailors' faces how their ventures had gone. Crabbing, like gold-mining, was one of the Bering Sea's biggest provisions.

The officer she had indicated approached, cautiously. She drew nearer as well.

She cycled through her memory bank. She didn't quite have a photographic memory. But it was a close-run thing. Details and information often stuck with her.

It was a gift and a curse.

She glanced back at Brenner.

She could remember the first time she had seen him drunk. He had only been fifteen. She could remember the first time she had realized his father had been beating him. Could remember the bruises. Could remember sneaking him into her parents' mansion, into one of the bathrooms to clean up his face.

Sometimes, she wondered if she would have preferred to forget such memories. But other times she was glad she couldn't.

She turned back towards the cop.

"Was anything found on the victims?"

The man had a thick beard. It was almost like a rite of passage in Alaska. Flannel and beards. Though Brenner had recently shaved.

Even so, the police officer extended something towards her. A plastic bag. And within, she spotted a wallet.

"Identification cards are in there," he said quietly.

She gave a polite nod, accepted the evidence, and turned back towards Brenner.

As she did, using the plastic sleeve to protect her fingers, and to protect the evidence from contamination, she pried open the wallet, gingerly. The sand crunched under foot, giving way to her steps. As she opened the wallet and looked within, she noticed it was mostly empty. There was a driver's license, mostly worn, and she managed to slip this free, studying it through the plastic wrap.

Both of the police officers were watching her curiously; there was still no sign of the coroner. A few of the dockyard workers were glancing over the wooden barricades, watching the police curiously.

She took a mental snapshot of the figures on the dock, cataloging their faces. Not because she suspected any of them. But because the more information she found, the better.

She hesitated, her mind drifting faintly into uncharted waters—she didn't consider herself a very prideful person. Then again, whenever she thought of her family, all she could really do was think in terms of pride. The pride they so often displayed, and the pride she had of not being like them.

It felt like a trap to think about her family.

But now, as she glanced back at the wallet, she held up the identification.

"Jeffrey Taylor," she said.

Brenner nodded. "Yup," he said. "That's the guy."

She looked at Brenner. "How long has he been missing?"

"Two years. He broke out of Anchorage Correctional Facility. Been on the run for about twenty months. At least, so we thought."

Brenner leaned in, peering into the cage, examining the bones within, wearing a disapproving frown.

"One of these looks like it's been here longer than the other," Brenner said.

"I noticed that too," Ella replied. "They're both picked clean though."

She said it matter-of-factly, as if commenting on something like the weather. But it gave her no pleasure in making the claim.

Both of them grimaced.

Brenner said, "Anything else in the wallet?" She opened it, glancing within. And frowned. Within the wallet, tucked in one of the sleeves, there was a five-dollar bill. Except it was encased in laminate. The thin film had protected it from the water. She unfolded the bill, through the bag, her fingers slipping from the slick surface of the two items. But she finally managed to extricate the bill, spreading it, and she stared at the markings.

"What is it?" Brenner said.

She waved towards him, and he stepped away from the cage to peer down.

There were words written on the bill.

No, not *words*. At least, not *only* words. It was a website.

She read it, slowly.

www.iamwatching.com.

She hesitated. "That's strange; what do you think it is?"

He paused. Then shrugged once and pulled out his phone.

Behind them, Ella heard the sound of a slamming car door. Approaching footsteps, and humming. The coroner had arrived by the sound of things.

She could hear other sounds, too. Deckhands being called back to their ship. The sound of straining ropes being lashed to the mooring posts. A third crabbing vessel was coming back; she watched as the water lapped against the metal hull.

But then, another, static sound caught her attention. She returned her gaze to the phone in Brenner's hand.

She stared down. The website was a simple one. A black background. No graphics. And a video player, front and center. Brenner clicked the play button. The white triangle turned to two white lines, and then the static grew louder

"What is that?" she said quietly.

A red timer suddenly appeared. Big, bold red numbers. *Three hours, twenty-six minutes and fifteen seconds.*

Fourteen seconds. Thirteen seconds. Twelve. Eleven.

She watched as it began to count down. And then, in the black box framed by the bright, flashing red numbers, the video began to show the image of a man. He appeared in frame under the red numbers.

The man was wearing a hood low over his features. His voice was muffled, and had a robotic quality, as if he were attempting to disguise it.

She couldn't make out much about the room the man was in. It looked strange. With a large, white pipe behind him. A boiler room?

She spotted nuts and bolts, riveted metal, and soldering all holding the pipe together. Besides this, nothing had been left in frame. No graphics or logos on the man's hood, either. And the red numbers continued to flash above his head. And then, the figure began to speak.

Chapter 4

The voice of the hooded man in the website's video player was still muffled, disguised. And as the figure spoke, the static grew louder.

"And so the game begins," the voice said, conversationally. Ella felt tremors down her spine at the first sentence. Something was so very off. Something that made her shiver and her skin crawl.

"I have been waiting a long time to play my game."

The man sounded depressed more than anything. His voice echoed. And he let out a long, rasping sigh, like a vampire waking from some graveyard after centuries of rest. "But now that we've started the game. There's only one way to stop it. This was birthed in love you know."

It was strange to try and listen to the words without being able to see the face. Without being able to see the lips speaking, the eyes moving. No facial expressions at all. Just a dark lump of shame. The appearance of a boiler room behind.

And then, Ella watched as the video finished.

But the countdown continued. The red numbers at the top of the screen continued to tick.

"Three hours until what?" Brenner said.

She shook her head, frowning. Her breath plumed on the air, caught by a chill breeze coming over the water. The two of them were silhouetted against the outline of the cold mountains, capped by snow. The sea itself was churning. Further from the shore, she watched where the water broke, turning white, and thrashing towards the beach.

Where the water hit, it spread, soaking into the sand and the shale.

"Whatever this game is..." she said.

Brenner frowned. He lowered his phone, pocketing it.

"Did that look like a boiler room to you?" Ella said.

"Maybe. Big pipe. Could've been one of the crabbing boats too. An engine room."

She hesitated and glanced at him. "Have you worked on one of those vessels before?"

He shrugged, took a step. As he did, she noticed the pronounced limp in his right leg.

"I've tried a couple of times," he said briefly. "Wasn't quite my speed."

The two of them were examining the skeletons in the cage again. Now, they heard the sound of footsteps behind them. Ella turned, glancing back. A grandmotherly woman wearing camouflage slacks and pink, woolen gloves was approaching. Doctor Tulip Messer was beaming at them.

As she drew near, her two silver earrings swished. Her smile widened further.

The last time Ella remembered seeing Doctor Messer, the coroner had a compound bow strapped to her back, having returned from a hunt in the mountains.

Dr. Messer was a woman that Ella respected. But she was also leery. Her father was one of Tulip's hunting buddies.

Ella turned cautiously, waving briefly.

Part of her felt a flutter of concern. Ella was still trying to determine who had been sent to kill her in her motel room the previous week. The only reason she *hadn't* been killed was because Mortimer Graves had got there first and killed the hitman.

But someone in Nome had hired the assassin; she had a very short list of *possible* suspects. And the coroner was on that list—in fact, Priscilla was also on that list.

But Ella kept her face impassive, like always. Her tone was pleasant, polite. She smiled and said, "Good to see you again."

Dr. Messer gave a chuckle. She had a small packet of beef jerky in one hand, and she lowered a stick of meat as she drew near. She said, "Nice to see you too, Eleanor. Brenner," she added, giving a nod and a smile. "Don't you two look so cute together."

Ella blinked. Brenner shifted uncomfortably. Neither of them quite made eye contact with the other. Both of them, Ella supposed, logged this comment under *things that grandmothers are allowed to say without reproach.*

As the coroner drew closer, though, she stared towards the cage, then she went still. Frozen in place. Stunned.

Ella could read the look of confusion etched across the woman's countenance.

"What's wrong?" Brenner said.

"They told me there were two bodies. They didn't tell me it was this."

"What's the matter?" Brenner said, a bit more insistently.

But the coroner had approached the cage now, peering into the crab pot.

She studied the skeletons, her mouth unhinged. And then she said, "That's incredible."

"What is?" Ella said, coming to Brenner's assistance in the questioning department.

Dr. Messer waved her hand. "Last week, I got something just like this."

"What do you mean?" Brenner said, his voice going rigid.

She said, "Exactly what I said. I found something just like this. Two victims caught in a crabbing pot. Both of them stripped clean."

Now Ella and Brenner were both staring wide-eyed at the coroner.

"Last week?" Brenner said.

"That's right; things were hectic with those kids going missing in the mountains," said the coroner. "So we haven't had the time to really work the bodies."

"Who was assigned to the case?" Ella asked.

"It was still being investigated by Chief Baker's detectives."

Brenner was frowning now. He shared a look with Ella.

"We're going to need access to those other victims."

"Victims?" said the woman.

Ella nodded, grim. She pointed to the padlock. "I don't think anyone would willingly sneak into a crabbing pot. But even if they did, this was locked from the outside. This was murder."

"We really need to see those two other victims," Brenner repeated, his eyes dark.

Chapter 5

It had taken nearly an hour for the coroner to complete her task, bag the bodies with the assistance of a couple of forensic interns that had arrived later, and then return to her office.

Now, Ella and Brenner were walking into a cold, refrigerated unit in the bottom of the precinct.

They'd come through the back entrance. The walls were gray, cold. A couple of pictures ornamented a desk in the far corner. Both pictures displayed hunting buddies.

Doctor Messer also had macaroni artwork which she had left framed on her desk. From her grandchildren.

"Cookies?" the white-haired woman asked, reaching for a bag left on the table.

Ella quickly shook her head. She had experience with Messer's cookies before.

Brenner, though, didn't stop to exchange pleasantries. He was already halfway across the room. Scanning the refrigerator units.

"Not there," Messer said. "There is no point. Like I said; they're picked clean."

She moved towards the metal closet on the other side of the room. Unlocked it, opened it. And then slid a gurney out. It was wider than a normal one might be. She pulled the sheet back, revealing two skeletons left on the metal surface.

As she did, she spoke conversationally, "A man and a woman," she said. "They were found just like those other two. As if they were embracing."

"Did you notice anything strange about the ribs?" Ella asked. "As if one had been stripped clean more than the other?"

The woman shook her head. "The size disparity isn't something from being stripped clean. Chronic pleural disease. Sometimes the ribs enlarge." She glanced towards Brenner. "Did your escaped convict have a medical history?"

Brenner nodded. "Yeah... Plural... whatever. Sounds right," he said, frowning, picking out his phone and studying it. After a bit, he said, "Yeah—looks like Mr. Taylor was suffering with rib pain when he escaped from the medical unit."

"I see," said Dr. Messer.

"Another couple," Ella murmured, staring down at the unfortunate figures on the gurney. The two skeletons had also been picked clean by the sea, the salt, the elements, and the fish and crabs.

She thought she could see marks on the bones where crab claws had nipped away, pulling, gouging, ripping.

She frowned as she stared down, her skin prickling. She thought of the video they'd watched. The threat that a game had just started.

Only two hours remained on the timer on that website. Ella glanced at her phone, frowning at the website which she couldn't stop checking.

She spotted a text bubble in her phone as she swiped away from the website again. The text bubble caused a jolt of fear to lance through her, and she knew why.

Mortimer Graves, the Graveyard Killer, had used the phone to text her as well. He'd been the one to contact her about the Spring Children in the frigid Alaskan wilderness. But she felt a sigh of relief as she spotted the text wasn't from Graves.

Rather, she hesitated, realizing it was from her younger cousin.

Madison Porter's *last* text message to Ella had been, *"Wanna see my missing toe? Cool right?"*

The newest one was simply, *"Hey... I have a favor to ask. No big deal, but do you have some time?"*

Ella stared at the phone. The two text messages summed up her younger cousin's personality completely. Madison was still only a Junior in high school. The young woman had been through more than many went through in a lifetime. Her father was sick. Her mother had died. She had been hunted in the mountains the previous week with her high school friends, pursued by a crazed serial killer.

Madison Porter had gotten frostbite and lost a toe, but seemed chipper about the whole thing as if it were something cool to bring to show-and-tell.

Ella sighed, feeling Brenner nudge at her. "Everything good?" he said.

She was frowning and gave a quick shrug. She returned her attention to the phone briefly, considering it. She liked Madison and had seen a lot of herself in the younger Porter. She wasn't exactly sure *why* Maddie and her father had come to Nome.

But her family's money had a strange allure, drawing moths to a flame. Maddie had nowhere else to go, and her own father was dying.

Undoubtedly, there was some hope that Ella's own family would take care of their cousin.

The last thing Ella wanted for Maddie was for her to fall into the clutches and under the influence of Priscilla, Jameson and Lois. Mom, Dad, Sister... the *true* owners of Nome's soul.

Ella texted back. *"Sure. Am at work. Let me get back to you."*

She sent, stowed her phone, then returned her attention to the bodies on the gurney. The coroner was watching her, and Ella turned her ever-present, pleasant smile towards the woman. Some people thought a mastery of one's emotions was weakness.

The ability to control one's temper, one's feelings... People who had no control of their own emotions resented her for her autonomy from them.

But in Ella's experience, emotions were useful tools, but cruel masters.

"Is there any identification on these two?" she asked simply.

"None," replied the coroner. "I've been able to identify the woman, though, based on dental records."

Dr. Messer turned, adjusting her fluffy sweater's sleeves as her camo pants made a swishing sound. She tapped on a computer resting by the gurney, pulling up a photo of an ID.

Ella leaned in. So did Brenner.

They both stared briefly.

Brenner gave a low whistle under his breath, and Ella found the sound irritated her, but she couldn't blame the reaction. The woman on the screen was stunning. Not just pretty, nor simply attractive. Her face alone, in a DMV photo of all things, was shaped like that of a super model.

The screen flashed with a head shot of a woman with long, vaguely curly hair, shiny and brown. Her eyes, lips, nose and cheekbones were perfectly set in a symmetrical oval face–her features matched each other almost to the millimeter. Centering the whites of her eyes was a glistening emerald gemstone in each pupil, and the lower-than-normal lashes looked like brushes. The corners of her mouth turned up in a slight smile and her eyebrows were raised just enough to make them appear natural, as if she were about to make an ironic comment about herself.

It was a coy picture, communicating beauty, but also communicating a knowledge of how to properly present one's self.

Ella and Brenner were both staring at the attractive woman for a moment. It was such a strange thing how something as superficial as meat on bone could so enrapture the mind.

Brenner looked away swiftly, shooting Ella a quick glance.

Ella said, "A model?"

"A news anchor," replied Dr. Messer quietly. "A small, local station."

"And that's her?"

Ella turned. So did Brenner, both of them looked at the two skeletons on the gurney, where they lay side by side. The bones of each skeleton were bleached and grey, lifeless, and yet the woman's face on the screen seemed to sparkle in comparison.

"Yes," Dr. Messer said. "That's her."

It was such a strange juxtaposition, Ella thought. But then she frowned.

Coming from a gold-mining family, she was all too familiar with how humans trained themselves to value appearance over true beauty. To concern themselves with glister and glamor and appearance.

These things were fine. Nice, even. Good, at times.

But they had no moral weight.

No benefit in and of themselves.

She thought, briefly, of her young cousin's words. *I lost a toe. Wanna see? Cool isn't it?*

Most young women wouldn't have been so cavalier, but Maddie had courage that most didn't.

Suffering produced it.

Ella had once heard Chief Baker's father, a type of minister—though she didn't know what type—say something that stuck with her. A verse, she thought. Or maybe some sermon note. The phrase had struck her as almost poetic. She could remember the cadence of it now... In many ways, she felt as if she deeply understood it.

"We rejoice in our sufferings... Suffering produces endurance, and endurance produces character, and character produces hope, and hope does not put us to shame."

Ella considered this briefly. "Do we know who the guy is?" she asked. "Not another escaped convict, hopefully?"

Dr. Messer shook her head. "No records. Can't take fingerprints, obviously. Dental isn't showing up. Off-grid type, maybe."

Ella nodded. "Makes sense. Lotta people in Alaska who like to avoid being found out." She looked at Brenner. "Any other escaped convicts you've been looking for?"

He shook his head. "Not recently. Not that we haven't got a bead on, at least." The man shifted slightly, preferring his left leg, his right hand massaging his thigh instinctively from his old war wound.

"Let's look into the woman, then," said Ella. "We'll probably be able to identify the guy that way. At least hopefully."

Brenner flashed a quick thumbs up. They took screenshots of the DMV photo.

Ella read the name out loud. "April-Beth Renee." She stared at the beautiful picture once more, feeling a pang of sadness. She felt like apologizing to April.

Then she sighed, shook her head and turned towards Brenner. The chill in the coroner's office was getting to Ella.

Four victims so far. Both of them found in crabbing pots. Both thrown out to sea.

And a creepy video on a card they were meant to find declaring two hours before this game of his continued.

Whatever this *game* was.

Ella wanted to scowl, but like always, she kept her emotions clear, her expression unreadable. She nodded politely to Dr. Messer, thanking the coroner.

She said, "Cause of death? Any way to determine?"

"Drowning," said Messer simply. "That's my best guess. No damage to the bodies except a few broken fingers on the guy."

"Torture?"

"No," Messer said, grimly. "I think it was when he came to and tried to break out of the cage."

Ella shivered again, turning now and moving away.

"Are you sure you don't want a cookie?" the camo-wearing, bow-hunting grandma called out.

"Thanks, we're good!" Ella replied.

Brenner snorted.

The two of them strode back out of the coroner's office, both of them glancing at Brenner's phone as he pulled up the information on April-Beth Renee.

Brenner was shaking his head. "All sorts of weirdos have been coming through Nome, recently," he muttered. "I think it's because of that stupid gold-mining tv show."

"What show?"

"Ah, it's on some history or discovery channel. Don't watch it myself. But a bunch of losers keep coming up thinking they'll strike it rich or something."

Ella nodded. "Gold attracts."

"So do pretty women," Brenner replied. "And my runner—he was a good-looking guy. For a convict. Probably had attractive women hanging all over him."

Ella paused. "You think the killer is targeting good-looking people?"

"Could be... at least part of it. But probably more than that."

"Not always more... but sometimes," Ella said, thinking once more of Mortimer Graves. She felt a lance of guilt as she glanced towards Brenner.

He was pretty in his own way, too. She didn't stare long, though—didn't want to be caught looking. Sometimes, she could feel Brenner watching her in the same way she liked to watch him.

The history between them wasn't something that would die overnight.

She moved now, heading towards the door at the far end of the long hall, leading away from the coroner's office.

"News anchor's offices are only a few miles north," said Brenner. "Near your parents' clean-up compound."

Ella frowned. Her parents had operations all over Nome. She shrugged, "Might be worth speaking to her co-workers. Does Ms. Renee have family in the area?"

"Nah. None," Brenner said.

He had a note of bitterness. She remembered the last time she'd seen him with his family. Cleaning up bottles outside his father's trailer to help out the man who'd beaten him as a kid.

Ella had never understood Brenner's loyalty to his old man. Brenner's dad was as bad as her own parents, just in the other direction. Using his misery and ill-fortune to spread it to others.

But Brenner still stuck around.

She admired him for it, and it also scared her.

Now, the two of them approached the parked car, moving quickly as Brenner programmed the GPS to take them to the news studio where their identified victim had worked.

Ella picked up the pace, feeling the cold chill of Alaska swell over her as winds came down from the mountains and over the salty sea.

The air held the fragrance of saline and goosebumps erupted across her arms.

And all the while, she could only think of that timer counting down. Ticking slowly.

They were running out of time.

And the most unnerving part was... when the clock struck 0... she didn't know what was going to happen.

Chapter 6

Brenner allowed Ella to take the lead. He didn't like stairs—they always pronounced his limp. And the elevator in the lobby of W-AT, the small news station, was out of commission.

He massaged his right leg as they reached the top of the stairs of the neatly maintained office building.

A pleasant reception area met their gaze.

The walls were painted a neutral cream, the floors and walls a red oak laminate that looked like stained hardwood. Modern abstract art hung on a few of the walls, with the lighting subdued, creating a warm glow. The desk was a dark, varnished oak with a phone. A few papers and a vase of fresh flowers gave the hard desk a softness.

An equally pleasant and warm receptionist looked up and over at them, waving her hand.

A girl, who was about twenty-some-years-old gave them a bright smile. She was plain, but pleasant. A bit on the other side of well-proportioned, but she wore her weight well and dressed with confidence.

"Hello," she said softly. "Welcome into our little corner of the world. May I help you?"

She spoke pleasantly, and her eyes twinkled as if in perpetual good cheer.

Despite his common dislike of strangers, Brenner found he instantly liked the young woman.

The two law enforcement officers approached the table. The woman glanced at either of them, her eyes lingering on Brenner a split-second longer before darting to Ella who was in the lead.

"How can I help you?"

Brenner watched Ella as she stepped forward. The twenty-eight-year-old woman didn't lean on the counter, but stood upright, shoulders set. Ever the professional. Brenner, on the other hand, slouched against the counter, leaning his right elbow against the cold marble.

The woman behind the counter glanced at him, holding his gaze a second longer. The sparkle in her eye turned to something of a mischievous twinkle as she gave him a quick once over.

Brenner hid a snort of amusement at the brazen ogling. Ella, on the other hand, didn't look as amused.

She was twisting her phone in her hand now, and Brenner's own amusement faded as his mind flitted back to the ticking clock on the website.

The strange man who'd disguised his voice and appearance wanted to play a game with them. Technically, Brenner's job was over. He'd found the escaped convict. Albeit, at the bottom of the ocean, stripped to the bone.

But Ella had been sent out to Nome as the only field agent, and she needed all the help she could get.

Not just from the locals, but her own family.

Besides...

Standing near her, it almost felt like the good old days.

Before he'd served his tours as a SEAL sniper. Before he'd gotten injured. Before he'd started drinking again.

He hadn't taken a sip since she'd been back.

He felt a warm flush spread across his cheeks at these considerations, and he desperately hoped Ella couldn't read his mind.

She was clearing her throat, polite as ever, one hand touching absent-mindedly to an unpierced ear. "We wanted to speak to you about one of your employees."

"Oh? Which employee?" said the woman behind the counter.

Brenner glanced at the triangular nameplate on her desk that identified this person as Kate Gardner.

Ms. Gardner had folded her hands in front of her. Her gaze darted to the side, though, towards a large, ornate, oak door set in the wall.

For a place like Nome, where most things were built for utility rather than luxury, the oak door with its swirling, wooden filigree stood out to Brenner.

The name on the door read, *Aspen Carmichael Jr.*

Some type of boss, probably.

Another door, behind the desk, read *Employees Only. Recording in Session.* A bright red light was blinking over this door. And a small television screen above the door displayed grainy footage of a news set where a teleprompter was being wheeled into place, last-minute makeup was being applied and the on-screen talent was practicing a series of vocal exercises that sounded like *me-me-me-me-me.*

Brenner smirked. He'd often thought actors and tv personalities were quite big on the word "me."

"April Renee," said Ella softly.

The woman behind the counter reacted as if she'd been slapped. Her eyes widened in surprise, and her lips opened faintly. She closed her mouth quickly. The spark in her gaze faded somewhat as if touched by the frost visible through the window in the wall the exit was set in.

A thin glaze of ice covered that window. And even through the glass, Brenner could hear the faint whine of the snow and the wind.

He took a step closer to Ella, not quite touching her, but standing closer.

He could remember a time in their youth, both of them teenagers, when they'd first started dating, how they'd often sneak off on one of Ella's father's snowmobiles and go sit on the dig equipment of his inland mining operation. During permafrost, the inland operation was closed.

They'd be wrapped in thick coats and gloves and occasionally chuck bits of ice down at the bulldozers, listening to the *clink* of the ice ricocheting off rusted metal.

Ella always climbed the dozers. She'd never been scared of heights. In fact, very few things ever frightened Eleanor Porter. No one would suspect it by looking at the woman. She was a frail thing. Only five-foot-two at most, with blonde hair and neat, pretty features. She used minimal makeup and most of her clothing was second-hand.

But she was an adrenaline junkie, and he'd glimpsed it on occasion over the years.

He could remember how she'd once tried to back up one of her father's sluice boxes in order to give them a precarious outlook over the metal fence circling the mining operation. She'd wanted to see the mountains, she'd said.

Brenner had joined her, if only to not be outdone. He'd been terrified, though, sitting on that precarious, cold, metal ledge, overlooking the mountains.

Ella, if anything, had seemed at peace.

No... she wasn't the scared type. Unless it came to the sea.

The ocean at large, and the seas surrounding the coasts were the only things that truly seemed to frighten Ella. She'd had an accident, years ago, out on the water, and had never really recovered since then.

Now, Brenner jarred to the moment, listening as the receptionist stammered. "I... I don't know anyone by that name."

Brenner frowned. Ella didn't, always the one with the poker face.

"Oh?" Ella said carefully.

Brenner took a more direct approach. "You reacted like you knew that name," he said.

She looked at him, and the mischievousness he'd seen earlier had vanished to be replaced by discomfort. "Umm... I... No, just it's..." she trailed off, leaning back in her chair now.

One of her hands was drumming against the wooden desk as if keeping beat to some unheard rhythm.

Ella, on the other hand, just watched carefully, frowning as she did.

Brenner said, "You don't know the name April Renee? She worked here. There are news clips online of her on that set." He pointed towards the screen over the blinking red light in the back of the room.

"Oh... Oh, you mean *April*?" said the receptionist, eyes widening as if just reaching some conclusion. "Oh... I thought you said..." she trailed off now, mumbling incoherently and staring at her hands.

Brenner and Ella shared a look, both of them quirking eyebrows. Clearly, this woman was hiding something. Maybe this case was going to be easier than Brenner had first assumed.

Things in Nome, Alaska were rarely easy.

The whining, cold wind through the thin window continued to remind him of this. It sounded like a faint whistling howl, an eerie, wraith-like catcall from the distant waters, ushering salty breath over rickety, insulated buildings and roads.

"I... I—maybe you should speak with the manager," the woman said finally, smoothing her shirt and trying to rise to her feet.

"You don't have to be involved in this," Ella said politely. "Just answer a couple of questions."

"And we won't detain you or arrest you. Maybe," Brenner cut in.

Ella sighed, but Brenner didn't blink, frowning now at the woman whose easy smile was now nowhere to be found.

Kate Gardner was now wringing her hands and shooting more concerned glances towards the door marked with the name *Carmichael*.

"April hasn't worked here in a month," she said quickly, whispering the words now and leaning low, as if to hide her lips, frightened that anyone else might overhear her.

"She hasn't? Have you seen her in that time?"

"No!" exclaimed Kate quickly, looking up again, wide-eyed. "Definitely not."

"You sound scared," said Ella carefully. "Is everything okay?"

It would not have taken an FBI agent to read Ms. Gardner's eyes in that moment, and Ella was now certain of at least one fact.

Everything was *not* okay.

Chapter 7

"It's... it's just," Kate Gardner stammered from behind her desk at W-AT, her voice dropping. "I didn't have anything to do with April. We weren't friends. Nothing like that. I didn't know she was poaching employees or... involved in anything like that."

She looked around the lobby of the small news station then back to the agents as if searching for their approval for her lapse in discretion.

Ella and Brenner shared another look.

"What do you think she was involved in?" Ella asked. Brenner nodded, impressed at the phrasing. Neither of them knew what the woman was talking about at all, but by phrasing it like this, it hid their own ignorance and offered Ms. Gardner a chance to prove her own knowledge, or even her own innocence. Gleaning information while feigning a position of strength. Ella was good at what she did, even though it was so subtle that most might miss it.

Gardner sighed, saying, "All I know is that she was found going through Mr. Carmichael's office late at night. We'd been having some issues. Two employees left abruptly to work for a competitor in Anchorage."

"I see," said Ella, "And so April was fired for soliciting these employees. What was she doing in your boss's office?"

Gardner nodded, her lips pressing together in a tight line. "I don't know. I don't think she was stealing anything. Maybe she was just... looking for something." She trailed off, wincing, clearly realizing this wasn't a very helpful answer. But she shrugged and said, "I don't know what she was looking for. I really don't."

Brenner and Ella exchanged a look again. It seemed like April Renee, as beautiful as she was, had been up to something, something more than just poaching employees. What sort of records might be found in a news station's office? Some sort of employee record? Business schematics? Leads on a big story?

Brenner frowned. In the end, everything so often came down to money. Who had it, and what they wanted to do with it.

"Thank you for your help," said Ella, offering a polite smile. "What did the other employees around the office think of Ms. Renee?" Ella asked.

"Umm... She was fine." Again, nervous, again her eyes shifting towards the ornate door. The woman shook her head. "I don't know. I didn't know her well if that's what you're asking."

"That's fine. Just casually. What did you think of her as a completely platonic coworker?"

Gardner bit her lip again, hesitating.

"I don't know," she finally said. "I guess she was okay. She was always... a little too bright, a little too ambitious. I mean, she was always asking questions and digging around. A little too curious for my taste. It made some people uncomfortable."

Ella and Brenner shared another look, and Brenner knew they were both thinking the same thing. April Renee had been getting too close to something. Something she shouldn't have been too close to.

But what?

Gardner suddenly cleared her throat and added, without prompting as if feeling a sudden spurt of conscience, "I... I think she was a bit of a loner," she said finally. "I think she was looking for something, looking for a way out. She was always asking questions, always trying to figure out what was going on and why. She wanted to make changes, I think. But no one was listening to her."

Brenner nodded, his brow furrowed.

Ella thanked the receptionist again and stood there, motionless, Brenner at her side.

Brenner's thoughts kept returning to the loner comment.

He glanced at Ella and something flashed in her eyes.

She knew exactly what he was thinking.

"We need to find what she wanted in that office," Ella said so quietly Brenner couldn't hear. She'd turned to face him, shielding her lips with a slouched head and raised shoulder. "We need to find out what she was looking for."

Brenner nodded. "Let's go," he said.

And, together, they set off towards the ornate, wooden door. Ms. Gardner tried to protest, her posture still tense and her eyes still wide. "He's in a meeting!" she called out.

But Brenner just waved away the comment.

Ella, on the other hand, was deep in thought.

"What do you think she was looking for?" Brenner asked as they drew near the door.

"I don't know," said Ella, her eyes narrowing in concentration. "But something got this woman killed. And she might have been a loner..."

"But she wasn't killed alone," Brenner said. "I was thinking the same thing."

And with that, Ella raised a hand, knocking quietly on the door. Brenner, on the other hand, feeling antsy now, also raised his hand and pounded his fist against the door, creating a loud, booming sound.

His skin pressed against grooves in the intricately carved, wooden door. Brenner stared at the carvings in the surface of the wood, discerning them to be in the shape and style of cave drawings he'd seen.

The rock art of southern coastal Alaska displayed such pictures and drawings from ancient peoples.

To see them on the wooden door caught Brenner somewhat by surprise.

The wooden carvings were an amalgam of animals, totems, and symbols. It seemed to tell a story, some sort of narrative, though he couldn't make out the exact details. In one spot, there was a mammoth chasing spear-carrying hunters. In another spot, there was a saber-tooth tiger with teeth sketched in silver, lounging on an outcropping rock made of gold leaf.

Brenner found himself temporarily entranced by the etchings, but then he heard the soft noise of footsteps on carpet.

There was the faint sound of a door unlocking, and Brenner and Ella stepped back, both of them turning to face the entrance.

The door opened and an aged man in a three-piece suit peered out. His face, though creased by time, was still strong, and his eyes sparkled with intelligence.

The man's eyes were the color of an evening sky; one was sapphire, the other emerald. His mustache was white and his long, wavy silver locks cascaded around a deeply creased face with a wide forehead, prominent cheekbones, and a pointed chin. His skin was lined from age, but not pale or sallow. It had the hue of honey and was marked with lines that told tales of many years passed.

"Can I help you?" he asked, his voice strong and commanding.

Brenner stepped forward and firmly shook the man's hand. He gestured to Ella behind him. "I'm US Marshall Brenner Gunn, and this is Agent Porter. We'd like to speak with you about one of your employees."

The old man looked them up and down, his eyes finally settling on Ella. He seemed to be studying her as if he was trying to read her every thought.

Finally, he said, "Come in."

The old man stepped back and opened the door wider, gesturing for them to enter.

Brenner and Ella glanced at each other, both silently wondering what they were about to find.

The old man led them into a large, airy room. The walls were lined with shelves containing books and old, framed pictures of news anchors, news bulletins and newspaper articles, and the floor was scattered with piles of documents and paperwork. Each pile was neatly arranged, but angled in haphazard directions in reference to the other piles, creating a sort of maze.

Brenner stared at it all. The man's own neat appearance didn't quite match the rest of the room's.

At the center of the room was a large desk, where the old man motioned for them to sit.

He took his own seat at the desk and began to speak.

"Now, what seems to be the problem?" he asked, his voice still strong and commanding.

Brenner and Ella looked at each other for a moment before Ella took the lead. They stood by the wooden bench facing the desk but neither took a seat. "We're here about April Renee," she said.

The old man leaned back in his chair and sighed. "Ah, April. Yes, I remember her."

He paused for a moment and then continued. "What do you want to ask? I can tell you what I know, but it won't be much."

Brenner hesitated. "You don't seem surprised we're here about her."

Mr. Carmichael just shrugged.

Brenner and Ella listened intently as the old man went on to explain, "April started out as a junior reporter at the station, but she grew increasingly curious about certain stories and had begun taking more initiative. She had been looking into a few stories that had seemed to be more than just news..." He paused, clearly aware he was speaking cryptically and clearly indifferent to that fact.

"What sort of stories?" Brenner asked.

The old man waved a hand, "Oh, you know... Stories. The types involving the key players in Nome." He flashed a knowing smile towards Ella then back at Brenner. The smile withered on his lips like an un-watered plant. He said, "She may have gotten into bed with the wrong sorts."

His eyes were cold as he stared at the two of them. "We've been told that she was found snooping in your office."

Carmichael didn't even blink, suggesting that this man also had a mastery over his emotions. He shrugged once. "An unfortunate incident. She was fired. It was as simple as that. I haven't spoken to her since." He leaned forward now, folding his hands in front of himself.

"Is she dead?" he said simply. "Because if she is, I can tell you exactly who did it."

He leaned back, looking smug, like a lion who's just taken down a gazelle but can't be bothered to actually consume the carcass.

Brenner felt a shiver down his back, and he frowned at the man.

"What makes you think she's dead?" Brenner said simply.

The old man shrugged, got to his feet, and gestured, "Let me show you something."

And he moved away from the desk towards a bookcase by the back window, he reached out to press on a book, sliding it into a groove, and then popping a hidden panel behind the shelf, sending a gust of dust scattering. He pulled the wooden panel, and, behind the bookcase, he revealed a top-of-the-line metal safe.

Chapter 8

Ella stared at the safe, wondering exactly what the contents would reveal about their super model of a victim.

Mr. Carmichael fiddled with the safe for a second, the device emitting beeping sounds as he entered the combination, concealing it with his body. Ella watched from the opposite side of the desk. The ornate, wooden door with intricate carvings had shut behind them, and she hadn't noticed when this had happened.

"This, I believe, should answer some of your questions," the owner of the news station said, turning to look at them.

In his hand, he held a small tablet. He approached them, setting the tablet on the table, swiping his finger across the dark screen, and pointing at the image.

"The security cameras from that night. Nearly a month ago—this was Ms. Renee's last day working for us, as I'm sure you can imagine."

"You didn't press charges," Ella said.

He just pointed at the screen as if to say *watch.* Then tapped a wizened finger against it.

Both Ella and Brenner stared as the tablet's screen illuminated, displaying the same office they were standing in, the same bookshelves, and the same files stacked around the room in what seemed a haphazard pattern.

It also showed the time, in digital green numbers in the corner. A little after midnight.

And that's when the door opened.

No sound.

But Ella watched as a figure wearing a hood slipped into the room, and she was briefly reminded—accompanied by a chill up her spine—of the image in the video player the killer had sent them.

Now, though, the figure's face was visible on the camera, despite the hood.

The same face of the woman who's DMV photo had been shown back at the coroner's.

April Renee slunk into the office, easing the door behind her, a thin strand of orange light severing as she shut the door once more.

Then a flashlight appeared, and a new beam of illumination spread across the room.

"She had a key," Carmichael said testily.

"Any reason she had a key from you?" Brenner said with a snort. "Pretty girl like that? She get a free pass to stop by any time?"

The older gentleman glared at Brenner. "It isn't like that. It never was. Just watch."

They did. The screen displayed the hooded figure of April Renee moving through the office, illuminating portions of it with her flashlight.

She was moving the light frantically, like some sort of lighthouse out at choppy seas, attempting to flag errant vessels to safety.

As she moved in the dark, grainy security footage picture, she looked frightened, on edge. Her shoulders hunched, her mouth open as if breathing rapidly. She kept looking over her shoulder towards the door she'd shut behind her.

She reached the bookcase and began fiddling with the books, searching--still—for something.

But what was she searching for?

Suddenly, the safe came into view, and the figure of April froze, her hand shooting out to grip the metal handle.

Ella leaned closer to the screen, her heart pounding as the figure hastily pulled a piece of parchment from her pocket, scanned the numbers, then entered them. She pulled the safe open and reached inside.

Ella's breath caught in her throat as the figure pulled out a small, lumpy bag, and stuffed it into her jacket pocket, glancing down to secure the item. She zipped the pocket, patted it twice, and only after feeling the reassuring lump of her ill-gotten gains did she suddenly seem to relax a bit.

She let out a soft sigh of relief, nodding to herself, then hastily shutting the safe, turning on her heel and moving rapidly back to the door.

And with that, she was gone.

Ella stared at the image of the door closing behind April Renee, her eyes wide as the implications of what she'd just seen sunk in.

April Renee had been a thief.

But why?

And why had it gotten her killed?

"She is dead, isn't she?" said the boss slowly.

The two of them looked up from the image.

He didn't blink. "A Marshal and an FBI agent show up at my small news studio, what else am I supposed to think?"

"You know that by showing us this, you give a motive," said Brenner quietly. "And if April also poached some of your employees, you had every reason to dislike her."

He sniffed, glancing at Brenner. "Employees like those aren't worth keeping. Besides, I have other recourse in such eventualities. I didn't press charges, but I'd already filed a civil case against Ms. Renee. You can check. In fact, I'm surprised you didn't."

His tone was hostile now, cold, and he slipped the tablet back into the safe, before closing it again with an emphatic *click*.

He shut the book back into its slot, then turned to face them again, his arms crossed over the chest of his three-piece suit. The old man's wrinkled features had drawn themselves into a look of disapproval which he levied on them.

"I had nothing to do with Ms. Renee's death. Showing you this proves *she* was the one who was up to something."

"And what did she take from your case?" Ella asked.

Now Mr. Carmichael smiled. He looked at her with the same expression a crocodile might use when eyeing a flitting swallow.

He said, "Now that's the interesting part, and the reason I decided to show you this video."

"What is it?" Brenner asked.

But now, the man shook his head and snorted. "You should know, if you work around these parts, that nothing in Nome comes free."

"So what do you want?" Ella asked, raising an eyebrow.

He glanced at her, "Assurances. You'll leave me and mine alone."

"Can't make that promise," Brenner replied. "We still don't know if you're involved in all of this."

The old man's lips twitched. "Then you'll never know what she took, will you?"

Ella and Brenner exchanged a look.

It was a standoff.

Ella glanced around the room, her mind racing as she tried to think of a solution. She had to get him to tell them what April had taken from his office that night, but the only thing she had to bargain with was their silence.

"Can I make you a deal?" Ella said finally. "We won't tell anyone what we've seen here tonight *if* it turns out you're innocent of involvement. We'll be subtle and quiet. If you're involved, we'll arrest you, but if not, we'll keep it from your competitors."

She trailed off. The implicit nature of her offer was clear as well. If he didn't agree, she was implying his competitors might find out. And for a news agency, that would be disastrous.

But she swept by the inference, allowing it to tinge his thoughts without fully curdling them. She said, "Just tell us what April Renee took from your office."

The old man considered this, his eyes narrowing as he thought it over. Finally, he sighed and nodded.

"You'll keep this silent, between us? And if you recover what she found, you'll give it to me?"

Ella nodded.

He shook his head. "I want one other thing?"

"What?"

"A meeting. A sit-down with your father, Eleanor. Yes, I recognize you. I know your sister. Everyone who's been in Nome long enough does."

Ella shifted uncomfortably but didn't blink. She didn't like the baggage that came with the Porter family name, but there was nothing she could do about it now.

The older man just looked at her, giving her a once over then said, "Deal? I'll tell you what she took if you arrange a meeting with your father."

"I can't promise anything," Ella said. "My father and I aren't exactly on speaking terms. The last time we chatted it was in an interrogation room."

She paused, frowning as she remembered the scene. A chaotic scene at night where Priscilla had nearly shot Ella. She frowned even more deeply. Someone... after those events, had hired a hitman to try and kill Ella.

Was it her sister?

Her father?

Someone else at the police station?

She shivered as she considered this. She knew Priscilla hated her guts, but it wasn't Cilla's style to get someone else to do her dirty work. At least, not when the work was personal.

Who then?

Her mind darted to her father, and she felt a chill down her spine.

She said, "I'll put in a good word." Her expression was a mask. Her voice similarly non-revelatory.

He looked at her, shrugged, then said, "I'll hold you to that." Then, he stepped towards the bookcase and opened the safe again, pulling out the same tablet he had before. He tapped it a few times, then turned it around to reveal a picture of a small, golden key.

"This is what she took from me. It is the key to a safe deposit box in the bank, a box that holds something very valuable. Something that I do not want in the wrong hands."

Ella and Brenner stared at the image, then back up at Mr. Carmichael.

"What's in the box?" Ella asked.

The old man shook his head. "That is not for me to say."

"Why not?" Brenner demanded.

"Because I don't *know* what's in it," he said simply. "And it's why I need a sit-down with your father, Ella." He glanced at her.

Ella felt another shiver along her spine. She stared at the man, frozen in place. "What do you mean?"

"Your father gave me that key five years ago," the man said simply. "Asked for me to hang onto it. I have... but someone else must've found out about it."

"My dad gave you a key?" Ella asked, wrinkling her nose. "Why?"

The man behind the desk folded his arms. "He said it was just in case. The key was only something he could use. But he needed me to hold onto it." Carmichael shrugged. "When the King of Nome makes a request, the rest of us usually don't ask why."

"So you've had that key, holding onto it for my dad for five years? And you never checked the safety deposit box?"

"Never. But April did."

"What?"

"I was notified by the bank three weeks ago." Now, Mr. Carmichael looked nervous as he paced back and forth. "They told me the box had been accessed. April Renee used the key to get the contents. Then fled. And now you're telling me she ended up dead." He shrugged, staring at Ella. He made a motion with his hands as if he were dusting them off. "I want nothing to do with any of this," he said simply. "I want to go back to my life, back to the news, and to be left alone."

"Wish more news people felt that way about others," Brenner said sarcastically, but he went quiet as Ella gave him a reproving glance.

She smoothed her blonde hair behind her ears, folding her arms as well. "So why do you need me to get a meeting with my father? If you two are so close?"

"We're not close. I did him a favor in return for..." The man trailed off, cleared his throat and shrugged.

"Another favor?" Brenner guessed. "The sort that gives him a bit of control over you? Are you being blackmailed by Mr. Porter?"

"No!" the news boss snapped. His eyes, though, looked guilty.

Ella frowned but hid the expression as if she'd simply been thinking. Her father had his hooks in all sorts in Nome. It was certainly like him to get ahold of someone who controlled the intake of news.

In fact, she would've been stunned if he *hadn't* had sway with Mr. Carmichael.

But now this left another mystery...

What was in that safety deposit box that April Renee took?

And why had April ended up dead, along with someone else... another male?

Her father was a dangerous man, and by the looks of things, the King of Nome was smack-dab in the center of all of it.

Four bodies so far.

A timer with only ninety minutes left on a blank, dark screen.

And Ella with a grim feeling that things were going from bad to worse.

"I guess we should go speak with my father," Ella said finally, glancing at Brenner.

The tall ex-sniper shrugged. He looked uncomfortable at the prospect of visiting the Porter estate.

He'd never been welcome when he'd been younger either.

She didn't relish the thought of speaking with Jameson Porter, but if her father had been involved in these deaths, if they were somehow tied to his business, then she needed to know.

She gave the old man in his office a final, cursory look, studying him, scrutinizing him. But then she frowned briefly, shook her head and turned away.

"Good day, Mr. Carmichael!" she called over her shoulder. "I'll put in a good word with my father."

"I didn't know that April had taken the key until it was too late!" the news man called out, his voice desperate. "Please... it wasn't my fault!"

Ella didn't reply.

She just gestured at Brenner and the two of them hurried from the office, stepping back out into the Alaskan air and inhaling the cool wind now gusting and whistling as it came in from over the waters.

As they made their way to the parked truck, Brenner was fiddling with his keys in one hand. His other, though, held his phone, which displayed the dark screen the killer had sent them.

They were playing his game.

Whoever it was.

And they had less than an hour and a half left to find out who was behind it all before the time depleted.

And then...

Who knew what would happen.

The two of them slipped hastily into the truck, and Ella had barely buckled before Brenner pulled away and sped back down the road, tearing through a thin dusting of freshly fallen snow as he sped in the direction of the Porter estate.

The chills along Ella's arms had nothing to do with the cold as she buckled her seat belt and stared through the windshield, her teeth clenched.

Chapter 9

As they slowly drove up the winding road to her father's estate, Ella could see the enormity of the majestic house perched atop the hill. It was larger than any other building in the area and had an air of authority about it.

The house itself was a sight to behold. It was a three-story behemoth with a terrace at every level. The walls were made of white stone and the windows were of a rich mahogany, reflecting the bright sunlight. The house was well-maintained and had a distinct feel of South-ern-style grandeur.

As Ella drove up the long driveway, she could see her father standing there on the terrace, wearing a silk bathrobe, peering down at her like a king watching his domain. He'd known she was coming.

This didn't surprise her in the least. Her father had eyes and ears everywhere.

Brenner shifted uncomfortably in the seat next to her, and she reached out, patting him on the arm in a comforting gesture.

Jameson Porter was a tall man. His features were sharp, clean-cut and shaven. He had his silver hair neatly arranged and he always smelled vaguely of sandalwood aftershave.

His face was handsome in the sort of way that seemed larger than life. The sort of handsome that belonged in a political ad. He wore a golden skeleton watch on one wrist, and his slippers were velvet, and his reading glasses, tucked in his robe, looked expensive.

She peered up through the windshield as they came to a halt in the driveway, beneath the shadow of his terrace, the shadow of his dominion. He didn't blink but just stood there, watching her arrive.

He was tall and thin with an air of sophistication about him. He wasn't moving, standing a floor above them, his arms folded in front of him, his neat hair ruffled by the occasional gust of frigid wind. He didn't care, though. Standing out in below freezing, he just looked down, his eyes as cold as the icicles dripping from the lacquered rail of his terrace.

He looked contemplative and emotionless as he watched his daughter emerge from the vehicle. She felt unsettled as she looked up at him. She didn't wave, though her instincts wanted to.

He moved then, slowly, turning towards the top of the stairs that led to the entrance of the house while he waited for Ella to arrive. She got out of the car and slowly approached him, feeling a strange mix of fear and excitement.

"Hello, Father," she said, her voice shaking at the thought of what he might be about to say.

He nodded his head. "Welcome," he said in a cool, calm voice. "I didn't expect to see you here."

She looked at him. Brenner was lingering behind her, having joined her, but staying a few paces back, as if he felt out of place.

Jameson looked her up and down. For a moment, she thought he might start yelling at her.

He didn't seem in any rush to step in from the cold. He wasn't even shivering, suggesting that, like she'd often suspected, her father had ice in his veins.

But then, he shrugged once and gestured at her with an imperious wave of his hand.

The gold tycoon stepped in through a door at the top of the stairs which he left ajar.

Ella winced, glanced at Brenner, shrugged, then took the stairs two at a time, the wood slick but still creaking under her footfalls.

She followed her father into the house, her mind a flurry of questions. What did he have hidden in that safety deposit box? What were the secrets he was keeping from her? She was desperate to know, but she had to remain calm and collected.

The inside of the house was just as grand as the outside. The walls were decorated with lavish paintings, there were heavy velvet curtains that hung from the windows, and the carpets were plush and luxurious. It all added to the feeling of mystery and intrigue that Ella felt.

Her father led her to a library at the back of the house and closed the door behind them. He took a seat in a large, leather chair and motioned for her to sit down. Ella did, her heart pounding in her chest.

"Isn't this much nicer Eleanor? Rather than dragging me down to a police station? Hmm?" He flashed a shark's smile at her, his hands folded neatly into the pockets of his bathrobe. Brenner stood in the doorway, having not been offered a seat. In fact, her father hadn't even glanced at him. Her father said calmly, "What do you want to know?"

Ella took a deep breath and looked her father in the eye. "We've received some news while looking into a case... We know you provided a key to Mr. Carmichael. And we need to know what you keep in the safety deposit box?" She spoke quickly, like tearing off a band-aid, not pausing even to inhale.

Once she was finished, she leaned back, like a poker player having rested their cards on the table in one, dramatic flourish.

Her father didn't blink. And again, his visage reminded her of a shark's.

Her father's face was unreadable. He looked her in the eye and said, "Carmichael?"

"Someone stole the key from him," Ella said simply.

"Who?"

"You don't know?" she said.

"No. Who?"

"You're sure you don't know?"

"Ella, if I'd known we were going fishing, I would've called for my boat. Why are you here?"

"I told you. What's in that box?"

"And I didn't tell you. So... I'd hate to think you drove up here just to leave so soon... I'd half hoped..." he trailed off and gave a supercilious sniff, "that perhaps you wanted to make amends."

She stared at him.

He stared back.

Ella felt her stomach drop. "Amends?" she said simply. She stared her father in the eye. Then, before she could stop herself, she blurted out, "Did you hire someone to kill me?"

Her hands tightened on the arm rests of her leather chair. Her father blinked once then he planted his slippers firmly on soft carpet.

For a moment, she glimpsed a flash of rage in her father's eyes. A rage she'd long known and had seen many times as a child.

A rage that gave his pallor a coldness that matched the frost on the mountain-facing window near the bookshelf.

Her father covered the expression as quickly as it had come. He smiled vaguely, waved his hand and said, "Now what type of question is that?"

She didn't look away. "You're not denying it."

"I am. Categorically," he said without missing a beat. "I would never, Ella. You're family."

She stared at him and found she didn't believe him. Not in the least. Her skin crawled as she watched her old man, and she felt as if her stomach was doing flips.

Was he the one who'd hired the hitman?

She had never been the best at reading her father. Priscilla was the twin who'd been closest to her parents. A daddy's girl, some had called her. Cilla Porter was set up to take over Porter Enterprises.

Ella, on the other hand, couldn't think of something that would entice her less.

"I can't help but notice," Ella said softly, "That you don't seem surprised that someone *did* try to kill me."

He frowned. "I am surprised, but also alarmed. And clearly, looking at you, I don't see any injuries." Her father shrugged, a flap of his bathrobe being smoothed modestly over his legs as he crossed them primly. He stared at her.

A living contradiction. Fury and a readiness for violence in that masculine face that didn't quite match the effete grace in the way he'd crossed his legs.

But something about the rage she'd seen flicker in his eyes kept her breathing in slow, shallow puffs.

At last, her father said, "Is that all? You've come here to insult me in my own home?"

"What was in that safety deposit box?" she tried again.

"Nothing to concern yourself with."

"So you admit there was something."

"I'm not admitting anything, Ella. I'd request you choose your words more carefully." Now, he'd pulled something from his pocket and was fiddling with it. He slid the item from hand to hand, and she realized it was a small, black, velvet bag with drawstrings.

The sort of bag that one might store dice in, or... in her father's case... ounces of gold.

She could hear the satisfying *clink* of small placer nuggets tapping against each other. Most gold now mined in Alaska was dust. It would be sluiced out in large sluice boxes, removed from pay dirt and gravel, then melted down.

But occasionally, amidst the flour gold, they would find nuggets. Rarely anything larger than a thumb. But even a couple of ounces of gold could pay most people's rent.

The small bag, small enough to fit in her father's hand, which he was hefting absentmindedly, would've been enough to pay a downpayment on a house in Nome.

She stared at the bag in his hand.

And he said, "This person who stole from me: are they using their real name?"

It was an odd way to phrase the question, but Ella just shook her head.

"April Renee, right?" their father said.

Ella didn't blink. She could feel Brenner tensing next to her. Her father spoke casually, but was watching them closely. "She was found dead last week, wasn't she?" her father said conversationally.

Ella crossed her arms. "You've been doing your homework."

Her father tossed the small pouch of gold up once more, catching it as it fell back into his hand. He nodded at her. "I have my contacts."

Ella thought of Dr. Tulip Messer. The coroner was one of her father's hunting buddies, but it irked Ella to think that the woman might have told Jameson anything about the case.

"So do you know April?" Ella asked.

He shook his head. "I never met her."

"She worked for a news agency."

"Yes."

"You did know her then."

"No, but I know of her. Now. She stole from my safety deposit box."

"And you won't tell me what was in it?"

87

Her father shook his head. "I don't see a warrant."

Ella said. "If I had a warrant, would it make a difference?"

Her father let out a soft little chuckle, tilting his head back to stare up at an ornate chandelier dangling from his vaulted ceiling. He seemed so at ease in that bathrobe, sitting in his leather chair like a king idling on his throne.

There were no armed guards, but Ella knew her father had men who worked for him who wouldn't be too far away.

"I think," Ella said slowly, "That you hired someone to kill me." It had nothing to do with the case, and she could almost hear Brenner Gunn drawing his breath shakily, but she just had to know... Had her own father hired the hitman? But this second round of fishing only yielded another blank, cold expression.

The wind was really picking up now, and she could hear it whining and whistling on the air.

Her father's eyes snapped back to her. He leaned forward in his chair, his gaze piercing through her.

"And I think," he said calmly, "That you have no idea what you're talking about."

But Ella wasn't so sure. She looked at the velvet pouch in her father's hands and thought of the gold nuggets inside. Her mind raced, searching for a connection between her father and April Renee.

"And I think," she said slowly, "That you hired someone to kill April Renee for stealing the contents of your safety deposit box. And that time, you succeeded. You had her killed."

Her father's face didn't so much as flinch. He simply stared at her, his eyes narrowed in contemplation.

"You'd better leave," he said at last.

Ella took a breath, bracing herself for his anger, but it never came.

Instead, he simply stared at her for a few moments, waiting for her to leave.

She rose from the chair but didn't turn to go. Not yet. Her father was involved in all of this somehow.

Men with this much wealth and power could be dangerous sorts.

Now, as she stared at him, her own mind racing, he leaned back in his chair, refusing to rise, refusing to show any fear.

The daughter and father faced each other in the quiet study, both of them under the magnificent, crystal chandelier.

Ella glanced up briefly, examining the ornate, golden chandelier. The chandelier glittered under the crystal glass globe that sat atop it. The gold was polished to a blinding shine. The crystals that hung from the frame like frozen raindrops glittered and sparkled in the light.

All of it designed to attract the eye. The glister, the spectacle, it made her frown.

She looked back down at her father, adjusting the sleeves of her second-hand suit she'd bought at discount.

She decided to try a new tactic. She didn't yet know if her father had hired the man to kill her. But she had the phone from the hitman shipped back to one of her partners. She'd done so after the Spring Children case, and she was waiting to hear back. If anyone could track the person the hitman had been in contact with, it was one of her old tech agents from her previous field office in the lower forty-eight. Agent Guyves wasn't the most conventional of operatives, nor was he a friend--not really--but he was a useful ally.

Still, she couldn't know if her father was involved for sure until she heard back.

And so she didn't know. She also didn't know if he'd been directly involved in April Renee's death. Nor if he'd had anything to do with the death of Brenner's escaped convict.

Four dead. Four found in crabbing pots.

And so far, her father was at the center of it.

Why had he stored a security deposit key with a news agency owner? What was in that safety deposit box?

Ella pulled her phone from her pocket, and she felt a surge of satisfaction at the way her father flinched, as if he half expected her to be pulling a gun.

But then, she turned her phone to face him, tapping the most recent tab and cycling to the eerie video, but this time... the image was blinking. It had changed.

She frowned, staring at the screen, her heart skipping a beat.

Chapter 10

The video was flashing. The red numbers buzzing. As Ella played it for him, silently, allowing her father to frown and listen, she realized the screen had gone fuzzy, and the numbers were shifting.

Again, the timer was ticking down. Only five minutes remained. The digital numbers on the black screen were now a bright, bold, neon red.

"What is this?" her father asked.

"You know," she said, firmly.

He looked her dead in the eyes. "I don't. What is it?"

This time, she found she believed him. Partly because she could read his expression now. Pure irritation.

"It is a game, apparently," Ella said. "A game played by this killer."

"The one who killed our little security deposit thief?" he asked conversationally.

"You're denying you had anything to do with it?"

Her father smirked, crossing a finger over his heart and raising a hand as if he were taking an oath. He then added, "In fact, I can prove it."

"How?" she demanded.

"Because I've been here," he said simply. "I run the business from home, nowadays, Ella."

"You've been here?"

"Yes. Right here. At home. On camera, in fact." He pointed up towards a security camera near the bookcase. Her eyes darted to it, narrowed, then moved back to her father.

"You expect me to believe you don't leave the house?"

"When I do, my driver takes me. And my guard."

"So you're saying you've got two men who get paid by you who'll vouch for you?"

"Yes."

Ella frowned.

"Whatever you might think of the testimony from my loyal employees, I can assure you, their word will hold up in a court of law. Between the footage here and their testimony... My days and nights," he added, "Will undoubtedly be accounted for. Do you have a timeline for when Ms. Renee was killed?"

Ella didn't reply.

"You don't, do you?"

She just watched her father. He seemed so smug, so sure. She felt a flicker of unease. Of course, she didn't think her father actually had pulled the trigger himself.

Though, according to the coroner, the victims had all died by drowning.

Her father hired people to do his dirty work.

But the way he was so casually offering an alibi made her wonder if perhaps she was wrong on this one.

Her father was involved, but perhaps he hadn't killed anyone.

As she thought about it, she felt as if the crabbing cages were a bit too dramatic for her old man.

He was a businessman, not a showman.

He wouldn't have wanted the attention. And tacking bodies into crab-cages with buoys was a surefire way to get attention.

No... no, perhaps he was involved but not guilty.

Still...

"I need a copy of your security footage from the last month, as well as the testimony of both your driver and guard," she said simply. "And mom's testimony too."

Her father snorted. "What about my livelihood as well? My soul while we're at it?"

You lost that long ago, she wanted to say. But instead, she simply said, "No, the alibi will do."

"Fine. I won't even make you get a warrant, my dear daughter. It's yours. I'll send the information along this evening. Anything else?"

Now, he rose to his feet also, and she noticed the way his hand strayed inside his bathrobe as if adjusting something near his waist on his left hip. She didn't doubt her father had a weapon concealed.

He was a cautious man, and he never entered an unknown situation without some plan.

She wanted to say more, but the way in which her father was willingly deciding to provide his alibi made her wonder if he had bigger concerns than the fear of being investigated for April Renee. Perhaps he knew he was innocent and had nothing to fear?

Or perhaps he didn't want a warrant or the feds breathing down his neck.

Her father's business had always come first, even if it meant he had to deal with hassles of his own.

Before she could comment on this, though, the screen on her phone caught her attention again.

The room grew tense. Her skin prickled.

Now, the red digital numbers had shifted once more. They were swimming across the screen like small worms wriggling.

The digital numbers tore apart a piece at a time, as some sort of animation created a strange spectacle on the dark screen.

Ella was about to say something when a voice suddenly spoke through the speakers on her phone.

The same voice they'd heard back on that cold, sandy beach outside the harbor. The same voice that had wriggled its way into her mind like small grains of cold, wet sand between her toes.

A voice that had a taunting, mocking quality to it, but also seemed to speak as if weighed down by the weight of the world. The voice let out a soft little sigh as it said, "We've only just started to play. I'd hoped for better... I really did."

The voice didn't laugh. Didn't chuckle. Didn't make the sounds that one so often saw in movies that depicted the psychotic and criminally insane.

No... No, this wasn't the voice of a man pretending to be unhinged.

This wasn't someone who had to *pretend*. No, this was a man whose actions proved his danger.

Like a lion who held back its roar in favor of prowling the night, looking for prey.

And now, that world-weary sigh echoed from the speakers again. Brenner, her father and Ella were all staring at the phone's screen.

The digital numbers were down to one minute.

And then, the remaining pieces of the number, the flashing lights all tore apart, swimming across the screen.

It was like watching red tadpoles swirl through ink.

But the animation--a cheap animation by the look of it--reformed.

Into two simple names.

The digital numbers had rearranged, the legs and arms of the numbers turning to letters.

And the letters simply read.

Hannah Bartlow. Amos Thompson.

And then there was a whirring sound, a digital beep. And the letters rearranged a final time to read *Game Over.*

The screen went dead.

Ella stared at it.

Her father looked up, frowning at her. "What sort of sick joke is this?" he asked, snapping, pointing an accusing finger at the screen.

He looked genuinely startled, genuinely irritated. The small packet of gold he'd been playing with was now abandoned on his chair where he stood next to it, glaring at her phone screen, then glaring up at his daughter's concerned features.

Brenner was at Ella's side, whispering the names. "Hannah Bartlow... I don't know her. But Amos... Doesn't Amos work for the *Three Dwarves?*"

"What's that?" Ella asked quickly.

Her father snorted in disgust, though, clearly having recognized the name. "A new establishment," he said, a scoff in his tone. "Only cropped up a few years ago. A yuppie thinks he's going to make it big among the gold-mining folk." Her father crossed his arms. "You know, during the earlier gold rush during the eighteen hundreds, the people who made *the most* money?" her father looked at her. "Not the miners, but the merchants. The ones who charged the wanna-bes all sorts of exorbitant prices."

"Thanks for the history lesson," she said, trying not to sound too sarcastic. "But what is the Three Dwarves?"

"A bar," said Brenner sheepishly. "Technically a strip club." He didn't quite meet her gaze but instead scratched at his chin, looking off through the window that faced the mountains.

The wind really was picking up now, and Ella could see gusts of snow being swept off the peaks and sent churning through the air, tumbling back towards the earth.

Ella said, "So this Amos Thompson guy works at the bar?"

"Owns it. Well... co-owns it with his sister," said Brenner.

Ella frowned at the screen. "So what's his name doing here?" she asked, tapping.

"I suggest you find out. After you kindly *leave my home*," her father said, his voice stern. He was gesturing towards the door now.

Ella looked at him, meeting his gaze. Neither of them flinched.

Ella nodded, her suspicions confirmed. Her father knew something about this game and he didn't want her to get involved.

"Okay," she said. "But I'm going to find out what's going on."

Her father didn't say anything, but his expression was clear. He wasn't happy.

Ella finally turned, and Brenner stepped out into the crisp morning air. They clambered into his old pickup truck, and the engine rumbled as they left the house and drove back towards the main hub of the small town.

Ella thought about the names they'd seen on the phone.

Hannah Bartlow and Amos Thompson.

Somehow connected.

Somehow involved in the same game.

And it seemed like it was up to her to figure out how.

"To the Three Dwarves," she murmured under her breath.

Brenner just nodded. She felt a flash of gratitude that he didn't bring up her accusations against her father. Didn't bring up her father at all. She had to put a pin in that line of questioning.

He was clearly aware of *something*.

She shot him a look. "Do you know this Hannah person?"

"No clue."

"Two names," she said. "A male and female."

He nodded, grimly. "Yeah. Two victims?"

She stared through the windshield, glancing out at the sea where the wind was picking up substantially. She watched as ice water clapped against the docks in the distance, sending jets of spray over the jetties.

Two more victims?

They'd run out of time...

But what did it mean?

And what was the game they were meant to be playing?

The wind whined and the engine groaned as they picked up speed, racing towards the bar owned by Amos Thompson.

Chapter 11

As she slowly came to, she shivered in the dark, a whimper caught in her throat. She could hear dripping and the clang of pipes around her like some eerie, ghostly organ music.

Hannah awoke in a cold, metallic room. She had no idea where she was or how she had gotten there. Her head was foggy and her mind was disoriented. She felt a chill run down her spine as she shifted against the strange, swaying floor.

She frowned, her head throbbing as her fingers probed at the metal beneath her, feeling cold rivets in an equally cold, metallic floor. But the whole room seemed to rock and sway, like a baby's cradle attempting to lull it to sleep.

But now, her consciousness returned, and sleep was the last thing on her mind.

Her mouth tasted funny. She licked at her dry, cracked lips, groaning as she sat upright, her back leaning against a tin-hued wall, her legs stretched in front of her.

The only light in the room came from a dim bulb hanging from the ceiling. She looked around, her fear growing with each second as she tried to make sense of her situation.

How had she gotten here?

Vaguely, she remembered last night... Remembered the figure sneaking up behind her.

Some man from the bar attempting to get her number, she'd thought.

But no.

"Amos?" she whimpered, her voice small and quaking in the dark. "A-amos? Are you there?"

Her eyes were adjusting to the dark as she blinked owlishly in the swaying room.

And then she realized...

She detected the saline scent, the odor of salt lingering on the air. The damp against her skin and the slosh of water tapping against the outside of the metallic walls.

She was on a boat.

Or, judging by the acoustics, *under* a boat. Having lived in Nome for seven years after her boyfriend had offered her a job, she'd grown accustomed to the sound of lapping water.

But how had she gotten onto a boat?

She groaned again, tottering, and trying to rise to her feet.

And that's when she felt the cold, harsh tug against her ankle. Pain flared through her, and she stared down, horrified.

A metallic manacle extended from her ankle into a bolted, soldered piece of metal in the floor, fastening her in place.

She was chained in the bottom of a boat.

"Hello!" she called out, now, her voice shaking, piercing the dark.

The single, flickering bulb above her cast her shadow across her own feet, and she blinked to try and adjust her gaze.

She swallowed, but the vibration at her feet caused her to stop the gesture halfway through, her lips still very much parched and cracked under her tongue.

The room was blank. Across from her, a porthole window, streaked with fog.

And there... at the far end of the room, a metallic staircase, leading up towards a door. This one shut.

She stared at the door, shivering.

No sign of a lock on *this* side of the door.

No handle either.

She felt a jolt of terror.

She'd heard horror stories about human trafficking. She glanced down, grateful—then terrified at the thought—that she was still wearing her old clothes. Jeans and a t-shirt under a sweater.

The manacle, though, reminded her that she was still trapped in place.

She bent down, her fingers scrambling against the cold chain as she desperately tried to pry it free, her breath coming in gasps.

Hannah, only seven years ago, after graduating from university, had been a track and field star. She moved quickly, her fingers nimble.

But it didn't matter.

Flesh always lost the war against metal.

"Come on... come on," she whispered desperately. "Fight through the pain. Through the pain," she murmured, trying to summon one of her own mantras she'd so often used in one of her track meets.

But now...

The words felt hollow, echoing in her ears the same way the swish of the waves did.

She glanced up as a new streak of moisture speckled the porthole window.

The light flickered once more.

And then, through the door, she heard a sound.

Footsteps.

Followed by the click of a key in a lock.

It was then that she knew.

She was in trouble.

She heard clanking from the staircase angled up and across from her.

Hannah's heart stopped. She could feel panic rising within her chest as she realized someone was coming down the stairs. She was trapped. She had no way to escape.

The footsteps drew nearer and nearer, and suddenly the room was filled with the dark figure of a man. His face was hidden in the shadows, and she couldn't make out his features. Fear seized her, and she scrambled to her feet in a desperate attempt to flee.

The chain rattled against the floor.

"Please!" she screamed. "Help me! Who are you?"

She tried to turn, to look for a weapon. There! A pipe at her back. Her fingers lunged for the pipe attached to the wall.

But it was too late. The man was approaching, and she could feel his presence drawing closer and closer. Her heart raced and her breathing quickened as she backed away, her eyes wide with terror. Her shoulder blades pressed to the pipe now, and she stared at the approaching man.

He reached out and grabbed her arm, and she tried to scream, but the sound died as his gloved hand cupped over her mouth, holding back her shout.

"Hush," he said.

And then he kissed her, on the forehead.

His fingers stroked her hair from behind her ear, running his gloved, leathery hand over her face.

Shivers erupted down her cheek. Waves of revulsion jolted through her.

He kissed her on the forehead—a gentle, doting kiss. An affectionate kiss.

She was pressed against the metal wall now, certain that her worst fears were coming to pass.

But then the man stepped back, his features still disguised in a hood. He stared at her, though, his eyes glinting in the dim glow from the bulb above.

"Do you want to play a game?" he whispered, standing a foot away from her.

He glanced down at where her fists were bunched at her side, both her hands trembling.

She looked up at him, swallowing and feeling as if she had glass in her throat from how dry it had gone.

She didn't have anywhere left to go.

She just felt waves of terror.

But he didn't give her a chance to reply.

Instead, he tisked his tongue, shook his head and said, "I bet you'd like to play a game, wouldn't you?"

He gave a little chuckle, nodding. Then, he reached into his pocket and pulled out something silver.

A knife.

She stared at it, eyes as wide as saucers.

He then gestured at her, pointing towards the ground. "Sit, sit," he demanded.

And he instantly slid to the ground, like a child at play time plopping themselves onto a foam mat. The man in the hood, in the dark outfit then crossed his legs, butterfly style under him.

He looked up at her eagerly, almost like some golden retriever in earnest desire for someone to play with it.

She stared at the man, her eyes the size of saucers, tremors shooting up and down her body as a panic attack flared through her system.

It took everything in her not to collapse.

But then, breathing slowly, she nodded and sat as well, crossing her legs the way he had.

What option did she have?

He had a knife.

And now, she looked at the knife.

"A Damascus blade," he said, smiling at her. "See the pretty, pretty patterns?"

His voice wasn't taunting, nor jeering. If anything, there was almost a sad quality to it.

He said, "I have a test for you, dearest. A game. How would you like to play?"

But she was just staring at the Damascus steel of the knife, which boasted an interwoven pattern of grainy swirls along with a light sheen that gave it an almost silvery appearance. In addition to the mesmerizing, river-bed patterns of the blade, the weapon also had a strange, jeweled handle. There was a golden ring attached to the base of the knife, looped through an open socket.

She glanced up at the man, still shrouded in the hood, and then back at the knife.

"What... what do I have to do?" she asked, her voice barely a whisper.

"Nothing at all," he said simply. "Just sit very, very still."

Then, he placed the knife on the ground and spun it, flicking his wrist.

She stared, eyes like saucers as the blade turned around and around. The knife point swept in a circle, the blade like a windmill.

And then, in this twisted, strange game of spin-the-bottle, the knife finally settled.

Pointing off to the left.

He giggled, the man rocking back and forth on his crossed legs, slapping his knees as if it were all good fun. He sat in the middle of the metallic floor as the boat continued to sway around them.

"Straight down the middle," he whispered. "Wow! Jeeze-Louis, what a rush. Let's try again."

She held back a yelp as he reached out, and then spun the knife again.

This time, the blade pointed directly at him.

He stared down, shaking his head and sighing. Then he reached for the knife, pulled it up, and pulled back his sleeve.

She stared in absolute horror.

There were cuts along the man's arms. Some of them old, scarred over, white ropes of skin against his wrist. Others far more fresh. Some bandaged, but others left open to the saline air.

For the first time, she heard a hiss of pain from under that low-hanging, face-shrouding hood. The shadow was aided by the angle of the light, which cast the shade of the hood over his features.

Now, the man pulled the knife across his wrist slowly, hissing again as he did.

The sound of pain was like ice down her back.

After a few seconds, he looked up again.

"Once more," he whispered.

He spun the knife again.

It began to slow, pointing towards him...

But then he chuckled and leaned in, giving a little blow with his lips, causing the knife to spin a bit further.

And once more, it pointed between them.

He let out a laugh, shaking his head then hopping to his feet.

"It's your lucky day!" he exclaimed, pointing at her.

"Three tries, and you're still here. Good for you," he said, and then he darted in.

She yelped.

But all he did was clap her on the shoulder, lean in and kiss her cheek.

"Well done," he said quietly, patting her on the cheek.

His voice was soft and sad and as gentle as a mother's caress.

It sent chills down her back.

But then the hooded figure with the knife turned, his wrist bleeding. Small droplets of crimson fell down his fingers as he turned away from her, moving back up the stairs, humming softly to himself as he strode away from her.

She stared after him, wide-eyed, horrified.

"P-please!" she said. "PLEASE!" she cried louder. "Don't leave me down here."

But he didn't look back. Instead, he tossed his knife a couple of times, like a child in a schoolyard playing catch. He walked up the stairs, playing with the blade, pushed through the metal door, and shut it behind him with a clang.

He left her alone in the base of the strange ship. Still disoriented, and full of terror.

What would have happened if the knife point had ended up indicating her?

She knew how to play spin the bottle. Had played it before.

Three times he'd spun that knife, and three times it had avoided her.

But what if it hadn't?

And would she have to play again?

She stared in the dull light, up the stairs.

And then, some laughter. "Let's play a different way."

The lights suddenly turned off.

She was left in pitch black.

And then, the *creak* of the metal door as it opened again.

And more footsteps this time.

Moving fast.

This time, there was no gloved hand to hold back her scream.

Chapter 12

Ella and Brenner pushed through the front door of the *Three Dwarves* strip club and bar. The rotating glass door swung behind them, sending a gust of wind through with them.

Ella and Brenner stood in a small atrium with a wishing well and a large, wooden-bead curtain behind a bouncer, which blocked the rest of the strip club from view.

Ella shivered briefly as the cold wind behind them swept in after them, but then was met by the radiating blast of a warm heating unit filling the space she now stood in.

Brenner nodded towards the bead curtain, and Ella fell into step.

But the two of them had barely made it two paces before they were confronted by a man built like an oak tree. The man was so large he nearly blocked the entirety of the bead curtain from view.

He wore a tight black t-shirt, which stretched across his broad chest, and a pair of jeans that looked two sizes too small for his frame. His face was expressionless, and his eyes were cold and piercing, set in a face that only a mother could love.

"ID?" he demanded without preamble. But then his gaze landed on Ella, and those mean eyes narrowed. "Ah, shit," he snapped. "You again?"

Ella blinked. She felt certain that there was no *again* between them. She'd never seen this man before in her life. She would've remembered.

Brenner stepped forward and handed over his own ID, but the giant didn't even glance at it.

"Nah. Neither of you are welcome," the big man said, his voice a bit higher than his frame might have implied.

Brenner snorted, then tried to sidestep. Ella moved cautiously as well, eyeing the man. "Federal business," Brenner snapped.

But the giant blocked their path, moving to prevent entrance and shaking his head. The bead curtain rattled behind him where his large shoulders brushed against them.

"Where the hell do you two think you're going?" snapped the giant.

He had to have been at least seven foot tall.

Brenner, a couple of inches over six foot, had to lean back to stare up at the behemoth.

Ella blinked as if she thought the man was a mirage. They were standing on the other side of a rotating glass door, just within the strip club.

The neon sign behind them illuminated the cracked sidewalk outside the club and glowed against the glass of the rotating door.

Now, though, the bouncer—who'd been sitting by a wishing well on a wooden bench—had risen to his feet to approach the two of them, his glower out in full display.

"We're here for a drink," Brenner answered calmly, not backing down.

"This ain't no place for the likes of you two," the bouncer said, his voice low and menacing. He gave them both a cursory glance, his eyes lingering on Ella.

She sighed. "Do you think I'm Priscilla Porter?" she asked, exhaustion falling on her.

The man snorted. "I know who the hell you are, bitch."

Ella waved away the insult, but Brenner scowled, stepping forward. "Watch it," he snapped. "She also happens to be an FBI agent."

But the bouncer just chuckled, shaking his head. "We told you and that cop husband of yours already. We ain't selling."

Ella stared, deciding now that perhaps this giant wasn't just a bouncer, but seemed to represent more of an ownership stake.

"This isn't Amos, is it?" she muttered to Brenner.

But the marshal shook his head and whispered back, his eyes still on the squinting giant. "No, it's his brother Eves."

"Eves?"

"What?" snapped the bouncer. "Stop your whispering. Get the hell out. Amos said no deal. So no deal!"

He was pointing an enormous finger towards the rotating door behind them. "You think we don't know you're the one who smashed my truck?" He sneered.

Ella winced. "I think you're looking for my sister," she said. "My name is Ella. Eleanor Porter. I'm not Priscilla."

"Bullshit. I ain't stupid. Now get the hell out."

But Ella had pulled her ID out. She flashed her badge, as well as her name. "See there?" she insisted. "Eleanor. I'm not Priscilla. She's my twin."

The giant was staring at her now, frowning deeply.

"We're not here to buy the bar. We need to speak with your brother, Amos," Ella said, keeping her tone calm, despite Brenner's agitated glances towards the big man. "We're worried Amos might be in trouble."

The giant blinked, staring at her, then her ID, then her again. He reached up, scratching at his chin.

"What typa danger?"

"Danger," Ella said. "And if my family had anything to do with intimidating you... vandalizing your truck, I'll personally help get them arrested. Deal?"

The giant didn't look convinced. But he glanced back at her ID.

"You don't seem like that bitch."

"I'm not Priscilla," Ella said primly, refusing to back down. The giant was easily twice her size. Perhaps even three times.

But she was stubborn with a smile.

And that smile remained affixed to her lips. Polite, confident and projecting an air of stubbornness.

Finally, the giant muttered. "I'll take you to Amos. But ain't letting you out of my sight." He then scowled. "And if you're lying..." He gave a little shake of his head then turned, brushing under the beaded curtain.

As he moved away, though, she caught a look on his face.

Worried.

Clearly, however big and intimidating the man was, he was concerned about his brother.

Ella and Brenner both winked at the other, then shrugged, then stepped past the wishing well, out of the atrium, under the wooden bead curtain.

The two of them stepped into the club, and though it was still early afternoon, Ella could feel the bass of the music shaking through her body. The air was thick with smoke and the smell of alcohol. Brenner put his hand on her shoulder and moved closer, as if he was trying to stay close to her in the midst of the noise.

A good number of the Nome denizens lingered on the dance floor but most gathered around the bar.

Lunch breaks in Nome were a sight to behold.

Very few activities, pastimes or watering holes provided much in the way of entertainment for the rough gold miners, fishermen and mechanics that often swarmed the shores of the off-beat town.

Rough faces and rough gazes watched them as the two of them followed the giant through the haze of smoke.

Ella kept her head held high, refusing to glance to the left or the right but keeping her eyes firmly ahead. The stages with the dancing poles were empty, currently. Likely on account of the early hour.

Ella didn't like strip clubs.

To her, it felt similar to gold-mining, though, she couldn't quite say why.

But there was a space in which people were no longer treated as people but rather as a means to an end that made her uneasy.

The giant led them towards the back of the club, pushing through a metal door, ducking as he did. He held out a hand towards them as if to keep them at bay, and said, "Wait."

Ella peered past him, into the small hallway the metal door led to.

Beyond him, in a well-illuminated hallway, she spotted a steel door that seemed to lead into a bunker. The door was clearly reinforced with soldered metal plates lining it. A thin slit in the top third of the door would allow someone to peer out at any newcomers.

But now, the sliding window in the reinforced metal door remained closed.

The giant leaned forward, tapping a fist against the door three times, pausing, then tapping a fourth time.

Then he waited.

No response.

He frowned, tried again. Cleared his throat and called out, "Amos, hey, it's me."

Still no reply.

Now, Ella could feel her own unease rising. She stared at the door, watching speculatively. The big man tapped his hand against the door once more, louder this time. His voice boomed over the sound of the pumping music behind them.

"Hey!" Eves yelled, "Open the damn door!"

But there was only silence.

Ella could feel Brenner tensed at her side. She also could feel the eyes of some of the customers behind them sweeping towards her.

Three men in particular, who'd been sitting around a circular, wooden table near the dance floor were glaring in her direction. The three men were all dressed like Alaskan fishermen, wearing oil-stained jeans, weathered boots and thick, woolen jackets.

One of them had a thick, bushy mustache.

They were all frowning towards her. She nudged Brenner, who glanced at them.

"Shit," he muttered.

"What?"

"Those are Reilly Oman's boys."

"So?"

"So," Brenner said quietly, "They're organized crime."

Ella tensed. "What?"

"Yeah," Brenner whispered, not quite glancing in the direction of the three men but keeping his voice low so they couldn't hear. "How do you think someone like Amos gets an upstart new club to take off in Nome without greasing some palms?"

"This place is a front?"

"Kinda. Oman's boys are assholes. No bodies yet but definitely some B and E."

Ella shook her head, feeling claustrophobic all of a sudden. The scent of the smoke around them continued to swirl, to linger and to cause her to hold her breath.

The three men around the round table were adjusting their woolen caps and rising now. The one with the facial hair scowled towards them and had his hand inside his pocket.

He was moving now.

Brenner remained tense, glaring back.

Ella tried to call towards Eves. "Excuse me, but is everything alright?"

The giant was still pounding a fist against the metal bunker door just within the unpainted hallway behind the club. He was shaking his head now, growling under his breath and muttering. "Come on... come on! Amos!" he yelled.

And then he turned, glaring at Ella and Brenner. "What the hell is this?" he snapped.

Ella paused, trying to gather her wits. Things were going sideways. "How about you let us try?" she said, stepping into the hall.

The three fishermen-looking thugs behind them were drawing closer.

Brenner had half-turned, giving them the stink-eye if only to keep them at bay. He flashed the weapon on his hip.

Ella didn't want it to come to shooting. She knew Brenner was one of the best shots she'd ever seen, but a gunfight was the last thing she wanted to instigate.

Her voice sounded pleading to her ears as she addressed the giant in the hallway by the bunker door. "Let's de-escalate, shall we? We can talk about this. We're coming in the hall, okay?"

She stepped forward, tugging at Brenner's arm and bringing him with her.

Then, she reached back and shut the door to the hall, sealing them off from the club.

The music faded to a dull pulse. The scent of ash and smoke still lingered, but it wasn't nearly as choking in the hall.

The big man had turned to them now and his eyes were wide with panic. Fear fluttered across his stretched, oversized features. "Where's Amos?" he demanded. "What'd you do to my brother!"

Ella held out both hands as if she were attempting to calm an enraged bull. "Nothing," she said firmly. "At all. We didn't do anything, sir. We're here to find him. Same as you. Does he normally answer the door?" She gestured past the giant.

But the big man was clearly starting to panic. His large hands had folded into fists and he was shaking his head wildly.

"You did this," the big man was saying, hyperventilating. "What'd you do? What'd you do!" he screamed. And then he lunged towards Ella with a shout, a fist flying.

Chapter 13

Ella moved fast, having already spotted the tensing of his muscles as the giant lunged at her.

She slipped backward, avoiding the first blow, but she felt the wind of the haymaker graze past her cheek, and a spurt of fear jolted down her spine as she realized if that blow had connected, it might have taken her head clean off her shoulders.

Her gun was in her hand now, aimed, pointing.

"Stop it, Eves!" she yelled, gun raised. "Hands in the air. Now!"

But the giant wasn't coherent. Tears were now streaming down his features. Something was off about the man. His eyes were bloodshot. Was he high? Unstable?

It didn't matter.

He was clearly frightened on behalf of his brother. And Amos, the name only familiar to her from the video their killer had sent, clearly wasn't where he was supposed to be.

The bunker door was still locked.

And the giant was clutching at his head with both hands. "You did this!" he moaned, his eyes still bloodshot.

Brenner held out a hand the same as Ella. Both of them were five paces away from the big man, backs to the door.

"Stop, now or we'll shoot!" Brenner snapped, his voice icy. He was trying to keep his own back braced against the door to the hall behind them.

For a moment, it seemed as if Eves had slowed. The giant was clutching his head in both hands now, as if he'd had a sudden headache and was shaking his head, moaning as he did.

Just then, though, behind them, the door echoed with the sound of thumping.

"Hey!" snapped a voice, "What's going on in there?"

Brenner cursed, leaning back and pressing his foot against the door jam, holding it in place.

Ella glanced again towards Eves, who was rising once more, scowling, tears streaming down his face.

Brenner kept his foot jammed in the door, holding it closed so the three thugs couldn't bully their way through.

But now, the pounding on the door was louder, and Brenner grunted as it shook.

"Shit, shit, shit," Brenner muttered to himself. He shot Ella a quick look. "Call for backup?"

Her phone was already in her hand.

But then it wasn't as Eves lunged once more, swatting it from her palm.

She didn't want to hurt the giant. He was clearly distraught if not mentally unstable.

But now, she stumbled back, her hand stinging. Her phone ricocheted off a plastic mop bucket against the wall. The mop in the bucket shifted, scraping against the cold concrete.

Eves was surging towards her. His fingers grabbing at her throat.

She fired twice.

Not to hit him, just to startle him.

The gunshots echoed by his ear, the bullets hitting the door behind Eves, shattering the lock on the bunker.

"Look!" she yelled. "Hey—look, the door!"

Eves hesitated, glancing back as the door handle to the bunker now fell off, clattering to the ground with an echoing sound.

Ella took this as an opportunity to lunge in and kick.

She caught Eves in the knee, eliciting a grunt as his leg buckled. She'd aimed for the joint, careful to use the man's own size against him, aiming to topple him.

Brenner tried to surge to her aid, but the moment he moved away from the door, it began to swing inward, pushed by the three Oman boys.

Brenner cursed and surged back, slamming his shoulder into the door, his blue eyes flashing as he grit his teeth and leaned into the door, keeping it closed.

Brenner was shouting now, but she couldn't make out his words.

She faced Eves, trapped in the tight hall, her shoulders set.

He was nearly two feet taller than her. Maybe three times her size. One of his arms was almost as large as her torso.

But she didn't back down.

Adrenaline spiked through her, and Ella could feel her body tensing. The same way it so often did during her pastimes. The hobbies that most didn't know about and rarely suspected someone who looked like her to engage in.

It was like standing in a plane, waiting to jump.

Ella took a deep breath and braced herself for battle. She stood her ground and looked up at Eves, her eyes meeting his. She noticed a flicker of surprise in his face, as if he was caught off guard by her, the small woman's, refusal to back away, but he quickly composed himself, massaging his leg where she'd struck and glaring at her.

For a brief moment, he tensed, as if trying to gauge the situation, but then he howled in anger.

His eyes moved away from the shattered door handle to his brother's bunker, and instead, he tried to lash out at her.

The giant surged towards her, but Ella was too quick. She grabbed the mop handle and swung it at Eves, striking him in the chest with a loud thud. He was pushed back by the force of the blow, momentarily stunned. She knew she couldn't let him get close.

The moment he laid hands on her, it was over.

Brenner would undoubtedly shoot the giant.

Eves didn't know it, but as long as he was losing the fight, he was safer.

If he started winning...

She shivered, certain it would end in blood.

But the giant kept coming, roaring now and swiping the mop away from his chest with a backhand.

Ella took this opportunity to rush forward and strike again, aiming for his legs. The mop handle connected with a satisfying crack, and Eves stumbled back again.

She darted away once more.

Moving in quick then back just as quickly.

Darting forward then retreating back.

The adrenaline was now pumping through her system, and a thin glaze of sweat dappled her forehead. She breathed heavily, excitement thrumming through her. Her eyes flashed, and she danced on the balls of her heels.

Eves was groaning now but tried to grab the mop bucket to chuck at her.

Ella pressed her advantage, swinging the mop handle with both hands in a fast and coordinated motion. For a brief second, she almost forgot herself. Her mind was conjuring images of her father. His cold, calculating glances. The encounter in his office, and his denial to tell them anything.

What had been in that safety deposit box of his? And had it gotten April Renee killed?

Ella's mind whirred as quickly as the mop handle; she landed several more blows on the giant, each one harder than the last.

"Stop fighting!" she yelled.

Her gun was holstered where she'd placed it, having decided not to shoot the big man.

She didn't want a death on her conscience. But now, Eves was slowing, groaning.

The door behind them, where Brenner braced, was still pounding. Voices were shouting.

"Hey, you in there!" a growling voice yelled.

Ella thought she heard the click of a gun, and tensed.

129

Brenner was still keeping the door shut.

Eves tried to lunge at Ella a final time, managing to wrap his banana-sized fingers around her leg.

She'd been distracted, and as he grabbed her, she yelled.

It felt like being caught up in the claws of some machine. He was just far, far too strong.

She fought desperately, kicking as he dragged her towards him where he hunched in the hall, gasping and recovering. She hit him again and again with the mop handle.

The wooden shaft shattered across his head.

She struck at the base of his neck like a lumberjack swinging an axe at a tree.

And then, her leg numb from where he gripped it, she struck him a fifth time. And only then did it seem to register to the big man that he'd even been struck.

He blinked woozily. Stared at her, tried to speak, but his words were slurred. And then, as she gasped, panic flaring, her leg on fire from his tight grasp—which had forced her to hop a few steps down the hall to maintain her balance—Eves' eyes rolled back and he collapsed onto the ground.

Ella had stood there for a moment, breathing heavily and feeling a sense of relief wash over her. She had done it. She had defeated a giant with just a mop handle.

What a rush.

Quickly regaining her composure, Ella grabbed the metal bunker door handle and pushed it open. Inside, she found a small room filled with computers, servers, and other high-tech gadgets.

Behind her, Brenner was shouting at her. "Hurry up! I can't hold them!"

Ella was moving through the small bunker room now, stepping over the shattered handle.

And then she froze, staring.

A window, reinforced with metal bars, had been broken. The metal bars were twisted as if they'd been melted away.

And there was blood on the ground under the windowsill.

She stared at the empty chair under the window.

Stared at the melted metal bars. At the shattered glass.

Her eyes narrowed.

She swallowed briefly.

"Brenner," she called over her shoulder. "Amos isn't here!"

"What's wrong?" he called back, grunting in exertion.

She peered down the length of the hall where Brenner's back was braced against the door, his foot jammed in the base.

She spotted a hand trying to reach through the small gap they'd created in the door, but then the hand yanked back accompanying a yelp as Brenner shoved even harder.

He was breathing heavily, sweaty, but holding his own for now.

The two of them met the other's gaze over the downed figure of the giant in the hall.

"What's wrong?" Brenner repeated.

She shook her head, glancing back towards the chair. The blood on the ground.

Someone had come through the window.

Someone had taken Amos Thompson.

She shivered, trying to make sense of it all, then shook her head. Her phone was in her hand as she placed a call for backup.

Amos was missing.

Someone had managed to reach a crime boss in his own bunker, behind a metal door.

Who was this killer?

Who was playing this game with them?

Ella felt shivers down her back, and she realized the cold, icy wind was coming through the shattered, broken and bent window.

Amos was missing.

She felt a bout of terror, wondering exactly what had happened to him.

She turned, her phone against her cheek.

Thumping sounds continued against the door where Brenner braced, keeping them secluded and barricaded in the hall.

Things were going from bad to worse.

And time was not on their side.

Chapter 14

Ella looked at the blood.

It stained the bare, concrete floor under the leather swivel chair. The various computer parts and electronics set throughout the self-contained room looked untouched.

"You see this?" Brenner muttered at her side.

She turned to look where he was pointing at the base of the windowsill.

The concrete had been cracked. A black spiderweb pattern extended down the gray surface.

She frowned, approaching.

Through the window, a gusting breeze whistled through. The cold wind caught her hair, ruffling it and kissing her face. She shivered, rubbing at her left cheek, her fingers trailing there.

Through the window, she also spotted the flash of red and blue lights. Police cars. Backup.

Chief Baker had sent the units fast enough, and now a couple of plain clothes officers were busily pushing the three men from the bar into the back of the SUVS.

An ambulance was there too, and Ella thought it was riding quite low to the ground.

Likely because of the size of the injured man it carried.

"See anything?" Brenner asked, casting his gaze about.

Ella just shook her head.

"He came through the window," she said simply.

"Well... yeah, that's pretty clear."

"He broke into a bunker to find this guy. Amos Thompson," she said simply. "He wasn't safe down here."

Brenner looked at her, scratching at his cheek. "No... I guess not." He watched her, allowing her to fill in the blanks.

But Ella had turned now to look at the desk in front of the leather chair.

It was scattered with pieces of paper—and the papers were blank.

The door behind them was shut. Another police officer had set up in the hall, acting as sentry.

For the moment, Ella and Brenner had the run of the room themselves. Brenner was pointing at the window.

"Our killer broke through there. Used a welding tool or something similar. No one heard him."

Ella jammed a thumb over her shoulder. The pounding music from earlier had faded now.

"Must've been during business hours," she said.

"Yeah, checks out."

"Shit."

"No kidding."

Ella said, "Who kidnaps someone from a bunker? And why Amos Thompson?"

"Dunno," Brenner replied. "What was the other name? The woman?"

"Hannah Bartlow," Ella said in a quiet voice.

"Huh. Still nothing on her," Brenner said quietly. "Maybe she's from the lower forty-eight. Just visiting up here."

"Or maybe it's a red-herring altogether," Ella said. She smoothed her hair back, feeling the way her thumb touched against sweat dappling her forehead.

Her left shoulder ached from where she'd fought with Amos' large brother. Her leg, which he'd grabbed, also felt like it had been put through the wringer.

The small, cramped bunker seemed impenetrable. The reinforced door. The metal bars over bullet-proof glass.

And yet the man who'd posted that video, the man playing this game had somehow managed to break in.

Without being seen or heard, and without alarming Amos himself.

"Why didn't Amos just run?" Brenner said.

"Hmm?"

Brenner pointed at the window. "When the killer was coming through. Amos would've seen him, yeah?"

Ella nodded.

"So why didn't Amos run?"

The two of them paused, staring from the window to the seat. The blood on the ground caught Ella's eye.

"Dead?" she said simply.

Brenner shivered.

"The coroner said that the killer was drowning his victims. Not shooting them."

"Maybe he had to make an exception this time," Ella pointed out.

She had moved over to the desk again, and was staring at the blank pages of white paper scattered across the surface.

The paper, she realized, had come from the printer, disheveled by the blasting wind.

She leaned in, adjusting some of the papers, placing them absent-mindedly back in the printer.

The desk computer was turned off.

She looked under the wooden desk, and then clicked her fingers.

"Hey, look--here."

Brenner joined her, bending down next to her. For a moment, the two of them peered into the dark space under the desk, and Ella felt the comforting warmth of Brenner Gunn pressed against her.

She felt an urge to jerk back, to distance herself, and then just as strong of an urge to stay right there.

Something about his warmth in the suddenly cold room gave her a sense of...

Hope?

No, that wasn't it.

Familiarity.

Brenner stretched past her, though, his fingers prying at the frayed mat she'd spotted under the desk.

Not quite a rug and not quite a bath mat. But somewhere in between.

And there, under it, she'd spotted the edge of a metallic rectangle.

"What is it?" she said as Brenner pulled the rug back.

"Just an electrical box," Brenner said, shaking his head. "In bunkers like this sometimes they come up from the floor to avoid compromising the stability of the walls."

He pulled a lip of the panel, opening it, and showing her a couple of wires meshed together by wire nuts.

She frowned, leaning back. Brenner let the mat drop into place.

For a moment, he stared at the side of her face. The two of them standing close, by the desk. She could feel his attention.

She could also see the blood on the ground.

Brenner cleared his throat, opened his mouth as if to speak, but she was already moving, hastening over to another side of the room where a rectangular black server was located. Blinking red and green and blue lights illuminated the black box.

She shifted the server a bit, expectancy rising within her.

"What is it?" Brenner asked.

She simply pointed at the cables on the ground in answer, directing Brenner's attention towards where they protruded from the back of the server and disappeared into a plastic sheath.

The wiring sheath moved along the side of the wall and deposited the same wires into the box under the desk.

"What?" Brenner said, hands on his hips now. He looked mildly irritated that she'd walked away from him.

She didn't react to his tone but instead pointed at the ground. "There's another panel here."

"How's that?"

She pointed again at a metallic corner visible under the server. She'd spotted it across the room.

"If this is just another electrical box," she said quietly, her finger trailing the plastic sheathe, "then why are the wires from the server, going all the way over to the desk?" She finished tracing the outline with her finger and looked up, quirking an eyebrow at Brenner.

The handsome marshal paused, blinked, then said, "Huh."

He hopped over the edge of the desk, grunting briefly as his right leg caught his weight, but then he strode to the server and pushed.

Ella helped.

Together, the two of them shifted it off the top of the metal rectangle.

This one was larger than the one beneath the desk.

And this one had a padlock securing it shut.

"Any chance you saw a key over there?" Ella asked, turning.

In response, Brenner tugged at her arm, pulling her a couple steps back, and then his weapon darted into his hand.

It was like watching lightning move.

The gun almost seemed a part of Brenner's arm as he raised it in one smooth motion and fired twice, aiming at the padlock.

The sounds of the gunshots echoed through the small bunker, almost deafening.

But the padlock was destroyed.

Ella stepped forward, wiping her palms on her jeans as she reached for the broken lock. She pried the metal pieces apart, which were warm to the touch.

As she did, she felt a shiver down her spine.

As she cleared the lock, Brenner opened the small box and inspected the contents.

Inside, there were two items.

The first one was a small, purple bag. She stared at it, recognizing it instantly.

She didn't need to see Brenner tug the drawstrings and reveal the gold within.

Her attention had already moved.

The second item within was a black box with a blinking light.

"What the hell is this?" Brenner asked.

"Some kind of tracking device," Ella said, taking it in her hand.

Brenner frowned as he watched Ella handle it. "I've seen Dr. Messer attach these to her ATV when they go on hunting trips. They're trackable even in blizzards. Supposed to be water proof. Cold proof. Everything proof."

She pulled on the side of the box, opening it, unlatching it.

And then, she stared.

Within, there was a single key.

Brenner and Ella both stared at the key.

"I never claimed to be a smart man, Ella," said Brenner softly, "But is it just me, or does that look like it might belong to a safety deposit box?"

Ella stared at the key inside the black, waterproof, GPS-located container.

Her eyes moved to the window.

It was all growing to be too much. It was all so confusing.

She stared at the window where a killer had come through. Stared at the blood on the ground.

Stared then at the safety deposit box in her hand with a key. The same sort of key that April Renee, their other victim, had stolen from Mr. Carmichael?

She looked at the bag of gold then at the key again.

Was this from her father also?

"What the hell is going on," Ella muttered.

And that's when the computer screen on the desk suddenly illuminated.

There was a crackling sound followed by the noise of heavy, echoing breathing.

And then a voice began to speak to them over the speakers resting on the desk.

Chapter 15

Ella whirled around to face the computer on the desk. She recognized the image nearly instantly. A dark, hooded figure sat in a shadowed room, streaming video onto the screen in the bunker.

"Hello? Are you there?" said the voice softly. "We've only just started playing, haven't we?"

Ella stared at the computer screen, watching as the hooded figure began pacing back and forth.

The man on the screen was shaking his head. The hood hung low, hiding his features. His face was hidden in shadow, and a single, sparking bulb illuminated the space around him, like a halo.

"Where's Amos?" Ella said firmly, staring at the screen.

At first, she'd thought the video was a recording, like the first one. But now, the man's head seemed to rotate when she moved, as if tracking her motions.

Shivers crept along her spine. As she watched the video, she tried to catalogue every pixel, picking out anything that caught her attention.

The man was in a new room now. A dark background, yes, but she spotted copper piping along the walls, and rust stains on the ground.

At least, she hoped it was rust.

The man's gloved hands clasped in front of him as he continued to pace.

"It's a difficult game we play," the man whispered, his voice disguised again. He shook his head.

"Where's Amos—" she began to interject again.

But he screamed, cutting her off, "SHUT UP! Just shut up!" He was breathing heavily now, his chest rising and falling under his dark sweater.

Ella could feel the cold coming through the open window behind her. She was still holding the small GPS box with the safety deposit key in one hand.

But her eyes were riveted by the computer screen.

"You don't take me seriously, do you?" the man whispered. "Hmm? No? This game isn't personal enough for you, is it?" He was staring right at her.

She could feel it.

The camera blinked above the computer screen, facing her.

She didn't look away.

The longer he talked, the better.

Brenner was on the other side of the computer, hidden from the killer's line of sight. His phone was in hand, and Brenner was holding a fiercely whispered conversation with someone.

Hopefully, someone who could track the IP.

Ella didn't want to draw the killer's attention to Brenner, though, so she returned her gaze to the computer screen.

"Who are you?" she said.

"You don't know me," he said softly. "Not yet. But there are those who do. It was all started in love, anyhow."

He nodded as if agreeing with his own words.

"What was started?"

"You know," he said simply.

"Where's Amos?" she tried again.

"Amos? You want to see Amos? Okay... I'll show you. See... see *I* told you what'd happen, didn't I?" If a voice could communicate a finger wag, his did.

And now, the killer was pacing.

He'd lifted up the camera on his hand, like a selfie, and was breathing heavily as he moved with it.

She struggled to reorient with the picture as it moved and swayed. Her hands were pressed on the desk as if glued to the wooden surface, braced there.

She watched as the dark image swam.

Brenner was still muttering feverishly into his phone, and she caught the briefest word of, "*Track it now. Right now, coming from the Three Dwarves!*"

She kept her gaze on the screen, though, watching as the figure moved.

Suddenly, the video image grew clear again. A new source of light illuminated the picture. All Ella could do was watch, tense. Her shoulder still ached, but she couldn't move, glued to the screen.

The man was breathing heavily still, but now he was saying, "You just don't understand how it works yet. But you will. Very, very soon. However..." He had a chiding note to his voice, almost like a disappointed parent. "It's worth mentioning," he said softly, "That there must be consequences, or you just won't respect me. That's true, isn't it?"

Now, the camera was facing something on the deck of a ship.

It took Ella a few moments to realize what she was staring at, but then, with a start that shocked her system, she discovered that she was looking at a crabbing pot on the deck of a water-slicked vessel.

Not much of the boat's railing was visible. But what she did see looked like rusted metal, worn by the salt and sea.

The man in the video stepped closer to the railing, and Ella felt her heart skip a beat. He was holding a knife in his hand.

The blade glittered in the light from the camera, and Ella felt her throat constrict. He was going to do something horrible.

Suddenly, without any warning, the man lunged forward and plunged the knife into his own hand. He twisted it, and then yanked it out. He didn't even emit a cry of pain.

But now, he held the knife up, showing it.

Red streaked the blade.

He chuckled, grinning and showing his hand towards the camera where he'd set it up.

Ella felt her stomach churn as she watched the man step back and survey his work, holding his fingers out in front of him. There was a nasty gash in his gloved hand, and blood swelled down his fingers.

"Consequences," he said simply. "Every good game has rules. And it all started in love..."

He was whispering to himself, his voice strained in pain. She could hear the howl of the wind, but this time it wasn't coming through the window, but rather seemed to be emanating over the speakers on the computer screen.

She heard something else.

Whimpering sounds. Desperate pleading. Voices lost in the cry of the wind but found again through the speakers.

Ella could barely make out the two black smudges inside the crabbing pot.

But she had a sinking sensation that she could guess their names.

Two figures were locked inside the metal container, both of them hunched, unable to stand fully, both of them desperately calling out, pleading.

Hannah Bartlow and Amos Thompson, she guessed.

The two names.

Now, the killer was shaking his head sadly, side to side. He clenched his bleeding hand tightly, the knife still gripped in his glove. "See?" he said. "I'm fair. I've always been fair. You just never understood, did you?"

"Amos! Hannah?" Ella called out.

Her words elicited a new round of whimpering from the cage.

The grainy footage, the sway of the deck suggesting the ship was out at sea, all of it made it nearly impossible to determine exactly what was happening.

But then she spotted the anchor. The killer was shuffling over to a spool of metal chain. An anchor resting against the rail.

The protests from within the crabbing pot reached a crescendo now. Desperation could be heard in those voices.

But there was nothing Ella could do to stop it.

All she could do was stand and watch, her mouth unhinged, her heart in her throat.

"One last kiss," he said simply, chuckling. "For the waves. A final farewell." He made a mock salute, one hand gripping at the chain.

And then he began to push at a lever.

The lever was attached to the chain, attached to a pulley.

The anchor began to rattle.

The voices of the two figures inside the metal cage were now drowned by the scrape of rusted metal against an equally weathered railing. The rising wind howled even louder.

The two faces inside the crabbing pot were suddenly visible, briefly, caught by the light on the deck.

A frightened woman with wide, terrified eyes. A man who looked like a smaller version of Eves Thompson.

Amos, no doubt.

The killer had been busy.

And quick.

How long ago had he taken Amos?

Why had he gone to such trouble? It almost seemed farfetched. Melting metal bars to reach a victim just to kill him?

What was even going on?

Ella had never felt so in the dark.

She felt as if she were playing a game without knowing the rules.

And the killer was now cranking the lever, dropping the anchor over the side of the ship.

Then, he pulled at something, and the anchor released. The chain began to unravel, making a thumping sound as each individual link clattered against the rail.

The two figures in the crabbing pot tried to protest. But then they were ripped away.

Ella watched, horrified, as the metal cage was yanked by the weight of the anchor through a gap in the railing where the pots would be released.

The two faces she'd been staring at became blurs of shadow. And then the pot was thrown over the edge of the rail, into the sea.

Ella shouted, desperately, lunging at the computer.

A second later, the image went dead.

Ella hyperventilated, frozen in place, gaping.

"What happened?" Brenner said. "Ella?"

"They're dead," she whispered. "We can't reach them... they're dead!" She was turning now, preparing to break into a sprint. There was no way to save them now, but what if the boat was close to harbor? What if they could recover the victims quickly? Maybe... was there a chance?

No. She knew there wasn't.

But she had to try.

Even as she began to bolt for the door, though, Brenner pointed, his voice hoarse. "Look!"

She did, only briefly.

And then froze.

Two new names had appeared on the screen.

Two names in the same digital pixelation as before.

Different names this time.

Matthias Baker. Priscilla Porter.

Chapter 16

Hannah screamed as the metal cage was thrown overboard. The fall into the Bering Sea felt like an eternity.

The rattling of the chain against the deck, the splash of the anchor.

Her heart leapt inside her, and she held back a shout.

She glimpsed, as they plummeted, the dark figure of the man with the knife standing on the ship, outlined against the rail.

And then came the splash.

The icy water swelled around her as she struggled to maneuver in the confines of the metal prison. The crabbing pot struck with the base first, providing some resistance. The surface area of the water caught the pot briefly, allowing it to submerge painfully slowly.

The cold, frigid sea swelled in around her. Hypothermia, she knew, would set in within minutes.

She could feel the weight of the water pushing her down, threatening to swallow her whole as it flooded in. A man lay unconscious next to her.

He'd passed out when they'd struck the water. She could see a gash in his forehead where his skull had struck the metal on impact.

But now, the water swelled up to swallow him.

Four feet. Six.

The water was now flooding through the bars. The surface tension of the sea had broken, the pot was tipping. The coldness was unbearable as it drenched her. Only her head was above water now, and she had tilted her chin, desperately gasping and spluttering salt water in order to draw greedily on the cold air.

All around her, she could hear the thrash of the waves, the whine of the high winds, the splash of the water against the metal hull of the old, rusted fishing boat which lurked behind her like the shadow of some great behemoth.

Her heart raced as she desperately tried to break free, her hands underwater, gripping tight against rusted bars. She pulled, pushed, tugged. Nothing. She could barely see now.

The water had passed her chin. Had passed her cheeks.

Swallowed her whole.

She was now submerged.

Small bubbles trickled from her lips as she held desperately onto the precious, precious air which was worth more than gold.

Air... such a strange thing to take for granted.

Her lungs were aching already. But this was perhaps from the penetrating cold.

She was going to die. She knew it, but she still fought. Hannah reached out with her hands, feeling blindly in the darkness for a way out.

The water thrashed around her, swirling, churning, icy and unforgiving. Her heart beat in short, choppy thumps as she struggled to keep herself oriented. Thick bubbles of air burst around her, fleeing pockets of her clothing, from under the cage as it descended, pulled by the anchor into the depths.

She could barely see anything. Her eyes stung in the dark water. Vague outlines of metal bars only seemed to taunt her.

She could feel the desperation growing within her. Her hands grasped at the metal bars, her nails scraping against the cold, slick surface. She tried to ignore the feeling of despair that was quickly creeping in.

Hannah didn't have time to glance over at the unconscious man lying next to her in the cage. She only spared him a single thought, wondering if he was being spared the terror. At least he would die at peace. She wished she could help him, but there was nothing she could do. She was too busy desperately trying to save herself.

She searched for something, anything that could help her break out of her prison. Then she saw it—a padlock.

There, securing the bars shut. For crabs, the lock would've been unnecessary.

But to keep them trapped down here... the psycho had gone all out.

But she hadn't come unprepared either.

Already, her free hand was yanking something from her waistband where she'd stowed it.

Even as the water pressure increased, battering her body as she plummeted deeper and deeper into the icy sea, and felt her head throbbing, her body gripped in the fist of the water, bubbles speeding around her, then fading. The trickles along her skin from the motion fading to a dull coldness... she still reached in her waistband and removed the item she'd managed to pry free back in her holding cell.

A loose piece of copper piping. She'd managed to tear it free while the psycho had been gone.

She'd wanted to use it as a weapon. But she'd never had the chance.

Now, though, she desperately jammed it into the padlock, scarcely able to see.

The only light had come from the ship above water, but now it was fading.

She had to move by touch in the sheer dark.

Wet, blind, entombed, like a child in a womb.

She continued to jab her metal pipe against the bars and then wedged it between two of the bars. She quickly adjusted her slick, soaked grip before the force of the water could take it away. With shaking hands, she felt the cold metal in her grip. She knew this was her only chance.

How much air did she have left? Seconds.

Her head was pounding.

With the pipe in her hands wedged between two of the bars, and jammed under the loop of the padlock, she began pushing with all her might.

Nothing happened.

She desperately tried to push harder.

How far down were they?

How far out to sea had they come?

She thought they'd struck the bottom of the sea bed now. The metal around her had jolted.

She nearly lost her grip on the pipe.

That would've spelled certain death.

It was too dark—she was absolutely blind, entombed in a mountain of water.

Her head was pounding horribly.

She knew there were rules about diving, about rising once the pressure had changed.

But they hadn't descended *too* far, which suggested they weren't in the deepest portions of the ocean.

Not shallow but not too deep.

Damn it.

Come on! she thought to herself, leaning on the metal. The rusted bars hadn't exactly been stable. The padlock was new though.

The pipe in her hand shifted.

Nothing gave. She struggled more, desperate, leaning with all her might at the bottom of the sea.

And then...

The padlock held firm, but one of the bars cracked. The rusted, old thing gave way to her insistent pushes.

She felt a flood of relief.

And she shoved.

She pulled herself forward, avoiding the jagged edges of the bars and thanking her lucky stars she was a small woman. The gap she'd just created...

Would it be enough to escape?

There was no sound as the metal gave way completely, the bar falling free, and Hannah felt a surge of hope. She frantically worked at the bars, prying them apart even further with the pipe, giving herself a bit more space.

She then wedged herself in the newly created gap. Her head pounded horribly. The air felt stale in her lungs.

She could see her life flashing before her eyes.

But she didn't slow.

There was no time to stop and die.

Not yet.

Her breath was gone. Dark spots danced across her vision—even darker than the black of the base of the Bering sea.

The cold was overwhelming. Her ears ached, and her jaw strangely throbbed.

But she tried desperately to wedge between the bars, and realized, in horror, she was going to have to empty her lungs to make it.

The fit was too tight. She had to suck in her stomach, to deflate, to blow out as much air as she could.

The only lifeline down here had been the air she'd drawn in. But now...

This had to go.

She could feel the terror threatening to constrict her, to hold her fast.

But she let out a groan and released the air at last, blowing hard and sending bubbles swarming up. Stale oxygen, carbon-dioxide, leaving her in pulses.

And then she sucked in her belly and once more tried to push through the gap in the bars.

It worked.

She squeezed through, feeling something tear along her arm.

But she didn't care.

The pain reminded her she was alive.

She kicked desperately, freeing herself.

She didn't look back at the man trapped within. The man she didn't recognize. She pushed off the ground, rising faster and faster, kicking desperately.

Her vision was gone.

All that remained was pain.

Panic swirled inside her as she rose through the liquid.

And then, above her, a flicker of light.

A glow, like the warmth of a candle attempting to entice a moth.

She burst from the water, her head emerging, droplets exploding around her.

She didn't even feel cold anymore, as if all her nerves had rebelled against the temperature.

She was next to the boat, floating in the cold water under the hull of the slow-moving, creeping vessel.

The shadow on the rail was gone.

She gasped, desperate, weeping now.

The tears streaming down her cheeks mingled with the liquid.

But she was still in danger of hypothermia. Still in danger of freezing to death.

She had to move!

She knew that much.

She kicked, desperately racing towards the side of the boat, but her movements were slow, encumbered. It was nearly impossible to scythe through the frigid liquid.

Her body was numb. Everything was numb.

But she put on a final burst of speed, using the churn of the water to propel her forward. If not for the direction of the lapping waves, it all would've been over, but she was due for *something* to not go horribly wrong.

A swell of the water allowed her to time a final kick, a final lunge.

She reached the underside of the large, rusted hull. Her hand latched out, and she maneuvered along the crusted, rough base, trying not to be broken against the metal as the water flung her against it.

She found the rungs of a Jacob's ladder. Relief flooded her. Her fingers could barely feel. She scrambled up the side of the boat. Desperate. Her ears ached, and she couldn't hear. Could barely feel.

Could barely see, but was still alive. She knew she needed to get warm.

But for now, she just had to get away from that cursed water.

She reached the top of the railing, peering along the deck, relieved to see the psycho wasn't there.

Where had he gone?

She wrapped her hands around the cold metal railing and pulled herself up. With one last effort, she made it onto the deck of the boat, falling onto the ground and emitting a wheezing sound.

She lay there for a few moments, shaking from the cold and exhaustion. She had made it out alive, but she knew her fight was far from over. Now, she had to find a way to get off the boat and back to safety.

The psycho still lurked on the boat.

And she was nowhere near civilization. No phone to call for help. No backup.

Just her on this rusted vessel with a crazed madman.

It was enough to make her almost want to jump back into the sea.

But she lay there, soaking against the deck.

The cold would kill her quickly if she didn't get warm.

She stumbled to her feet now, looking desperately around for a way to save her life a second time.

She needed warmth.

Then she needed to hide before the madman found her again.

Chapter 17

Ella stared at the two names on the screen. Matthias Baker. Priscilla Porter.

And another countdown.

Ten hours this time. Not long enough. Not by a longshot.

She leaned back in the front seat of the truck, staring at the image on her phone, watching the countdown tick away. Brenner was on the phone, speaking rapidly, urgently. "No," he was saying, as he broke every speed limit, racing through Nome's outskirts, heading towards the docks, "No—that's not right. I'm sending the link now. It's real. It's credible. Make sure they're protected. Yes—I'm serious!"

Brenner slapped his hand against the steering wheel, his voice rising. "Yes, dammit! *The* Chief Baker! Now! And his wife. Mrs. Porter—that's right. Hurry. Send three. No, make it four cars! Go now!"

He hung up, breathing heavily, scowling through the windshield.

"Where are they?" Ella asked, shooting him a sidelong glance.

"At one of your father's dig-sites," Brenner replied, still scowling. He shook his head. "You'd think you'd be able to reach the Chief of Police."

Ella frowned. "Are they going to call you back when they're located?"

"Yeah. Yeah, they should."

Brenner tugged at the steering wheel, veering into a side-street, hastening rapidly towards the docks which were visible in the distance.

The docks against the gray waters of the Bering Sea resembled a graveyard of forgotten ships, the sun setting in the sky. Old, rusted hulks had come in as evening waned.

The countdown continued to tick away on Ella's phone.

"We're almost there," Brenner said.

Ella nodded and grabbed her phone, sending a quick text to her father. She'd considered avoiding his number.

And for a moment, she paused, her fingers hovering.

She didn't want to involve her father, but if anyone could locate her sister and brother-in-law, it was Jameson Porter.

So she relented, grit her teeth and texted rapidly.

As she did, she noticed a little speech bubble above her thumb where her cousin, Maddie, had tried to get in touch again.

But Ella ignored the distraction, texting:

"Dad, please tell Baker and Priscilla to stay where they are. Cops are coming for them. They'll be there soon."

She hit send and looked up at the docks, hoping that they would make it in time.

She felt a strange unease at the sent text. Communicating with her father in any way was difficult, especially since she didn't know how he was involved in all of this.

But she'd seen that video.

The strange man in the dark hood with the knife.

He'd killed two more people.

And she couldn't do anything about it.

The truck skidded along an asphalt road, slipping across white-painted lines along the ground.

Ella and Brenner barely waited for the vehicle to come to a stop before hopping out into the parking lot.

The wind was still rising, and standing this close to the water's edge, the air buffeted around them, disheveling Ella's hair and ruffling at her clothing.

Still, she was moving rapidly, head low, Brenner at her side.

"Where are they?" Brenner said.

But Ella pointed. In the fifteen-minute race from the Three Dwarves, she'd been the one to call for the Coast Guard.

Now, she spotted where the Coast Guard cutter was bobbing up and down next to the jetty. A single officer stood in the boat, waving them over. Lights were flashing along the rail of the boat, and the multi-angle propellers were churning the water behind, mixing with the splash and roll of the waves.

Ella and Brenner hastened forward, their feet thumping against the wooden dock.

They had to hurry. Already, the Coast Guard was using GPS to track any vessels still out on the water.

"He's got to be out there," Ella muttered as she inhaled deeply.

They'd come to a halt by a rope wrapped around a mooring post. Brenner was already untangling the rope.

The coast guard was reaching out a hand to help Ella into the boat which they would use to find the killer's ship.

Ella ignored the hand, hopping into the vessel, and reaching out to grab the rail as the boat rocked under her feet.

Now, standing in the cutter, she realized just how tall the waves were, agitated by the wind.

The water was choppy and tumultuous, and Ella squinted her eyes, her gaze scanning along the horizon, looking for any sign of the killer's ship.

Brenner was speaking to the Coast Guard officer, and the officer had already started to guide the boat away from the jetty, the vessel's engine roaring as it started to move. The rope Brenner had untangled slipped over the rail, spooling on the ground like a wet, furry serpent.

Ella looked out at the massive expanse of the sea, her eyes searching for anything on the horizon.

They had to hurry.

The killer was out there. She'd already given up hope of finding the most recent victims alive.

Hannah Bartlow and Amos Thompson.

Two more dead.

Six victims in total, counting Messer's original two.

And the killer wasn't done.

The clock was ticking—the next targets were Nome's sweethearts. Chief Baker and Priscilla Porter were two of the most well-protected people in Nome, and yet the killer had called his shot.

Brazen, bold, audacious...

Whoever this murderer was, he'd managed to solder through a metal window to kidnap Amos Thompson.

He'd planned it all, and he was only just getting started.

The boat swayed under her as Ella moved towards a radar by the Coast Guard officer.

The man was short but strong, with thick muscles along his arms, his gaze focused on the screen.

"There," he said, pointing to a small, green blip on the radar.

"That's the boat we've been tracking."

Ella felt her heart race as the cutter sped towards the blip.

"What ship is it?" she asked.

"A crabbing vessel," said the officer, nodding. He wiped a hand along the radar, clearing flecks of water. "Isn't registered. We don't know what it is."

Ella frowned at the small green blip.

"Any other ships out there?"

"A few—but they've been identified. Three more are coming in to dock on the eastern jetty."

"Do we have officers waiting to search them?"

The coast guard nodded once.

Ella turned her attention back to the single blinking, green dot on the radar. A flash of a white line circled the screen again, and again, like the second hand on a clock face.

It was now or never.

They had to catch the killer before he could hurt anyone else.

Her stomach tightened as she thought of the images from the screen.

Two victims trapped inside a crabbing cage, thrown over the edge of the ship.

The horror of it still gave her goosebumps.

She glared now, peering over the radar, her hand braced against the rail, looking across the water.

The waves continued to rise. The swell of the ocean lifted like the humps of some great sea monster.

The cutter gouged through the liquid in a steady, white, frothing churn, angling in the direction of their suspicious ship.

"Just because it isn't registered doesn't mean it's our guy," she said, cautiously. "Any way to get drones out looking for others?"

The Coast Guard officer shook his head. "Inclement conditions. The winds are too high."

Even as he said it, the boat rocked, caught by a sudden blast of water, a wave sweeping towards them from the side.

A rogue wave. She'd heard stories—many of them—of how rogue waves, twice as large as most waves—would come unexpectedly and wipe out smaller ships.

Now that she was on the water, her hand tense on the rail, her own memories were coming back.

She had always hated the ocean. Ever since she'd been a teenager.

Now, scything through the dark water, she felt her stomach twist. She tried not to stare at the waves. Tried not to think back to her accident as a teenager. She'd nearly drowned.

She could feel the blood leaving her face as terror came to visit.

"Come on..." she muttered.

The ship rocked from the effect of the wave but they continued speeding forward.

She watched as the cutter readjusted and veered towards the blip on the radar, her knuckles white around the rail as the boat rocked in the choppy waters.

The air was filled with tension, and Ella could feel Brenner's gaze on her, but she was too focused on the blip to take any notice. Ella's grip on the rail tightened, her knuckles whitening.

The cutter moved forward, despite the rogue wave.

The green dot on the radar was getting closer.

Closer.

The cutter was getting nearer to the suspect vessel.

Ella glanced back, feeling the cold spray of the ocean mist on her face.

The wind was whipping around them, the sea rolling and cresting.

The boat was moving faster, and soon, the outline of the ship became visible, the hull of a boat a grey blur against the skyline.

The cutter was almost there.

Brenner was speaking to the Coast Guard officer again, and the man nodded, lifting his radio and speaking into it quickly, before turning back towards Ella and Brenner.

The cutter was almost there. The vessel on the horizon materialized in view, as if mountains were parting.

It was old and worn, its paint chipped, and the wooden decks were warped and splintered. The metal railings were rusted.

Ella couldn't tell if this vessel matched the one they'd seen on the video. The footage at the time had been so grainy.

"Think this is it?" Brenner asked, his voice a whisper.

Ella just shrugged, shaking her head and staring as they drew alongside the floating rust bucket.

Ella felt her pulse quicken as the Coast Guard officer cut the engine and the cutter came to a stop, gliding up alongside the crabbing ship, bumping faintly against the hull.

She held her breath, waiting for any sign of life on board the vessel.

But there was none. No movement. Only cold, motionless rails.

"It has to be it," Brenner was saying. "It's an abandoned ship. This *has* got to be the right boat."

The Coast Guard officer drew out his gun as he waved towards the Jacob's ladder.

Ella turned to Brenner, gesturing at the ladder.

He winced, rubbed his hand against his right leg, and then the two of them hastened forward while the Coast Guard officer kept their cutter steady.

Ella reached the ladder first, spray cold against her hands as she began to clamber up it, climbing towards the top of what appeared to be an abandoned ship.

All around her, it seemed as if everything moved and swayed with the water, with the high wind.

Darkness was filling the horizon as clouds came and evening fell.

She shivered, her teeth chattering as she clambered up the rungs.

The deck was sea-worn, the paint all but peeled away to the bare metal, almost the same shade as the ocean. Steam had puffed into the air as if ice were still melting away in the hold.

The deck was slippery and wet, cold and dark.

She stared along the barren space, her eyes moving to a stack of crabbing pots secured with zip ties against one side of the vessel.

A metal tank, like a wishing well, centered the heart of the vessel, where the crabs would be kept and unloaded during a fishing trip.

She frowned, swaying with the motion of the ocean.

No sign of any other movement.

No sign of anyone.

She felt a creeping sensation of fear wondering where the two victims were.

Directly under the boat?

Or had they drifted now?

She hated to admit it, but it would take a long time to find the cage with the two newest victims.

Her heart thumped.

Ella gasped as she felt Brenner's hand on her shoulder and she turned sharply to face him.

Words died on her lips, though, as she realized Brenner was pointing past her towards an open door in the deck.

A yawning, dark door as if it meant to lead them into some pit of hell.

Ella shivered, goosebumps ran across her skin.

"Think we should check in there," Brenner said. It wasn't quite a question, nor a suggestion.

Ella grimly bit her lip. She and Brenner both had their weapons in hand now, the metal flecked with droplets of sea water.

Brenner tried to protect his own weapon from the abusive spray as he crept forward towards the opening in the deck, like a trap door.

There was no sign of blood on the deck. No sign of the anchor or the crabbing pot with the two bodies.

No cameras. No hooded figure.

Were they even on the right boat?

Ella shivered.

The vessel itself was deceptively large. Most of the hull was under the water, laying low. Perhaps, even, she guessed, it was the size of a sideways apartment building. Not a large one, maybe only six floors... But still large enough to give her a sense of unease as she reached the hole in the floor.

Brenner paused, his hand darting to his phone. He stared. "Shit—I'm getting reception."

"What is it?" she asked.

She could hear the faintest sound of a ringtone over the howl of the wind and the slosh of the ocean, over the clang of their footsteps against metal.

Brenner raised the phone, handing it to her.

She frowned and answered.

"Sis?" snapped Priscilla Porter's irritated voice. "What the hell, Ella? You want war? I'll give you war, you bitch! You think you can get these goons to lock me in my own car! Are you insane!"

Ella winced, weathering the tirade for a few moments. She waited until Priscilla seemed to have calmed a bit.

For a moment, standing by the open trapdoor, facing a dark entrance and a metal stairwell that descended, Ella was relieved to have an excuse *not* to venture under the boat.

Still, being shouted at by Priscilla wasn't on her list of priorities either.

Ella said, "What are you talking about? Calm down, Priscilla."

"Calm down? You want me to calm down! Why the hell am I being forced to stay here? Huh?"

"Where are you?"

"The Indian River site," snapped Priscilla, her voice temporarily crackling over the phone as if the reception had suddenly worsened.

Ella noticed, as she glanced at the device, to make sure the call was still connected, that Priscilla's name was stored in Brenner's phone simply as "Priscilla."

Ella wasn't sure what to think of this.

Not Mrs. Porter. Not an unnamed number. Just... Priscilla.

Something very familiar about it.

She frowned, but then raised the phone again, refocusing. "Cilla, listen," Ella said, trying to cut into another acerbic tirade. "We need you and Matthias to stay put. There's a killer looking for you."

"What?"

"A serial killer. He's been targeting couples. Or... at least, two people at a time. And he said he's coming for you next. He says he'll do it in the next ten hours."

A pause. Ella felt a flash of relief. It was a rare thing for her sister to be at a loss for words.

"What the hell did you do?" Priscilla demanded.

"Nothing," Ella returned, speaking loud to be heard over the din in the background. "We just need you to stay put. I'm glad you're safe, okay?"

Priscilla swallowed. She didn't seem to know how to respond to this last comment. Ella was surprised she even said it. She was equally surprised to find she meant it.

For whatever else Priscilla was, they were still sisters.

The idea of a killer reaching her twin and her brother-in-law made Ella's skin crawl.

She glared into the dark hole and the metal ladder leading into the guts of the ship, now. A rising sense of anger filled her.

"Hey, just stay put, stay safe. Let the cops keep you alive, okay?"

A sigh. "How serious is this?"

"Very."

"God dammit, Ella."

"I have to go."

"And another thing!" Priscilla began yelling once more.

But Ella hung up, handing the phone back to Brenner. She shifted on her foot once, gave Brenner a long look, and then took a step into the trapdoor, down the ladder, moving into the cold dark.

Chapter 18

The ship echoed around her, moaning with the rocking and rolling of the waves, groaning in protest to the sweeping wind.

Her feet found hard floor, tapping against the metal.

Ella's breath came slowly, and she exhaled shakily as she took another step.

Her mind flitted back to the scene in the video, witnessing in her mind's eye as those two poor souls were thrown overboard.

Brenner stepped forward again, the light illuminating darkness.

The beam spotlighted a metal arch, copper piping along the wall. It showed stains of moisture on the ground and ceiling.

"We don't have any registration for this ship?" Ella asked softly.

Brenner just shook his head, a step ahead of her now, half-crouched, weapon in hand, flashlight gripped in the other.

Watching Brenner was like watching a surgeon in his element. Everything about the ex-sniper seemed poised and ready to go, stepping forward in the dark, one foot after the other.

His gun seemed an extension of his arm, and his shoulders were set.

He took solid, confident steps into the deeper portions of the vessel, moving down a second set of metal stairs.

"There are a few floors," Ella said, gritting her teeth. "We can't search all of it. He might just move."

Brenner said, "We have to try."

But she was already shaking her head as they moved along the first level under the vessel. She peered into a room. Empty.

Brenner pushed the door of another room open, his hand against the cold, iron frame. It displayed a porthole overlooking the ocean.

But this room was empty as well. In one corner, Ella noted a section of piping was missing. Strange...

And then there...

"Is that blood?" she said sharply, moving into the dark.

Brenner pointed the flashlight towards where she had stopped, shining the brightness at her feet.

Ella knelt, her knee pressed against the cold flooring, one hand still holding her weapon.

There, along the ground, she spotted a stain of red that stood out against the slick floor. Not rust...

"Blood," Brenner confirmed behind her.

She shivered, rising to her feet again. "I guess we're in the right place."

The boat swayed as if in response to this comment, and Ella caught herself, her hand against the porthole window.

Once the rocking had subsided, the two of them moved through the dark again, taking cautious steps forward.

But it was nearly impossible to see everything. She hadn't realized just how large the vessel was.

It felt like searching all the units in an apartment building with only the two of them.

If they missed anything, there was no telling if their suspect might just slip into a previously searched room, hiding and waiting for them to leave.

They moved cautiously in the dark, trying not to miss anything, searching room to room.

At last, having swept all the empty, lonely rooms of the first level, they moved down a flight of white-painted stairs to the next. A cargo area, by the look of things, though Ella wasn't familiar with ships.

The deeper they went, the more the feeling of dread rose in her stomach.

She liked challenging her nerves but facing a fear like this?

She would avoid the ocean for as long as she could for the rest of her life.

The idea of being trapped in a cage, thrown into the darkest deep.

She shuddered.

Again, the two of them moved through the dark, avoiding something that looked like a large boiler, and other spare crates or metal containers scattered through the larger space on this level.

A few more rooms were searched. Two doors, however, were locked.

Brenner and Ella paused in the dark, the flashlight illuminating the curved, L-shaped door handle.

Brenner frowned and tried again, but it remained locked.

He shot her a questioning glance.

Ella cast about for a key, but none was in sight. Brenner raised his weapon, pointing it at the lock, but then he caught himself and lowered it again.

"Ricochet," he muttered, shaking his head and kicking at the slick, metallic wall to make his point.

She nodded in agreement.

For a moment, she leaned forward, resting her ear against the door, her cheek resting against the cool metal.

She listened, and it was like hearing the heartbeat of the vessel.

The creak and groan of the floating metal thing...

But no sounds she could discern beyond that.

"Dammit," she muttered, leaning back and staring at the locked door.

Brenner tried the handle of the second door, a few paces to the right, and this one was locked as well. A stray pipe skittered along the ground where his foot caught it, and the sudden sound startled her, causing Ella's heart to jump.

Once she'd noted the source of the noise, though, she looked at Brenner.

"Now what?" she said.

"Gonna have to come back with backup," he replied.

She frowned. "We'll need someone to watch the boat."

"Yeah. Can call it in. Any news from Baker?"

She shook her head. "No reception down here."

"Priscilla was pissed, sounded like," Brenner said, staring at her.

She paused.

For a brief moment, standing in the dark, facing the tall, handsome man with those cold blue eyes, she found that her mind wasn't dwelling on her terror of the ocean.

For that brief moment, she just looked at him, studying his face, his jaw. A single burn mark traced under the side of his chin, up to his left ear. He scratched at it, absentmindedly, watching her with his solemn, blue gaze.

"You have Cilla's name stored in your phone," she blurted out.

Instantly, she shook her head and turned. "Sorry, sorry, never mind."

She was moving now, back towards the stairs. They would have to reach the deck, radio in for backup, and find a way to breach the doors.

Someone was possibly still on the boat.

Or maybe the killer had long since escaped.

Still... it was time they didn't have to waste.

Brenner followed after her, though, his footsteps in her wake. "Wait, what?"

"Nothing."

"Priscilla? Yeah, I mean. I have her number. It doesn't mean anything."

"Of course, I'm sorry. I shouldn't have said it."

They reached the white stairway, taking the steps quickly, both of them somewhat out of breath as they moved.

"No, hang on," Brenner said, snagging her arm when she reached the top of the stairs.

She turned to look at him. His flashlight pointed at the ground between them, casting something like a lunar glow.

"What?" she demanded.

"Are you mad at me?"

"No. No, I'm worried about finding this guy. I'm worried about Cilla."

He looked at her, scratching at his chin. "Huh," he said simply.

"It's nothing, Brenner."

"Mhmm," he said.

She studied his face, her eyes lingering on different portions, memories coming back to mind.

She thought about what he'd admitted. How he'd kissed Priscilla. The two of them had been an item after Ella had left.

She didn't know why it had made her so mad.

But it had.

Now, though, standing there, she wasn't sure what to think. Perhaps it was the fear. The rational part of her mind tried to reason with her subconscious.

Terror had a way of making a woman do stupid things at times.

And her terror of the ocean was palpable.

It felt as if part of her psyche wanted to escape into more pleasant memories. Like a person in pain opening a good book, looking for a temporary reprieve.

But as she stood there, staring at him, she felt a wave of jealousy.

She didn't like the sentiment.

And so she instantly rejected the feeling.

"It's nothing," she repeated, trying to turn again.

But Brenner didn't release his grip on her arm.

She turned back. "We need to hurry."

He just watched her, something almost lupine in his gaze. Brenner had always been the prettiest man she'd known. Now, his tall form was somewhat ducked to avoid the low-hanging metal joist above the staircase.

It created a sort of shadow along his features. And the glow of his phone wavered briefly.

"Brenner," she said firmly. "We need to hurry."

"You're shaking."

She looked down. Where he held her arm, not tight, but not too softly either, she realized her fingers were indeed trembling.

"It's the ocean, isn't it?" he asked softly.

She winced. She didn't want to talk about it. But then she just nodded once. "Can we go?"

He didn't release her. "You're terrified of the ocean. I know it. I've seen it."

"Sure. But this is where the case took us. We need to go, Brenner!"

"I don't want to. Not yet."

She blinked at the presumption. "Well..."

"Some of us," he said simply, his voice still lupine, his gaze like a wolf's, "go after the things we want. Not all of us live our lives in between spaces allowed for us by good manners."

"What does that mean?"

"It means..." he said, sensing the waspishness in her tone now and smiling at it.

And then he leaned in.

It was a surprising, jarring motion.

He almost seemed to maneuver with the boat. His lips touched hers, pressing against her. She felt a thrill down her body. A shock along her lips, a tingling buzz that spread.

They kissed, holding each other in that moment, and Brenner finally released her arm.

She didn't pull back.

Part of her wanted to turn and run. Part of her wanted to call for backup.

But in that brief moment, in the heart of an abandoned ship, even now realizing what a strange scene it must have looked, she kissed him back.

And then she pulled away.

He blinked, staring at her. And for a moment, it almost looked as if he'd been plunged into ice water.

"I... I'm sorry," he said quickly. Then added, "I'll delete Priscilla's number from my phone."

She looked at him, breathing heavily, feeling the flush along her face and chest. "No," she said simply. "Not yet. We need to make sure she's okay first. Now come on."

She didn't mention the kiss. Acted as if it hadn't even happened.

She turned on her heel, moving rapidly away.

After a few moments, she heard Brenner's limping gait fall into step behind her.

Her skin still tingled. The ocean wasn't as scary as she remembered. Though the fear was still there, lingering somewhere in the background.

But as she moved towards the top of the deck, she made a quick beeline towards the rail, to call out to the Coast Guard to radio in a new boat and backup.

It would take time to search the vessel properly, to get the tools to break down the door below.

Time they didn't have to waste.

If the killer wasn't here, then Priscilla and her husband were still in grave danger.

Chapter 19

Brenner scowled as the Coast Guard brought him to shore, and his eyes fixated on the horizon, looking in the direction where they'd left the rogue crabbing vessel on the choppy waters.

A second Coast Guard boat had arrived by now, and three officers were disembarking to help search the ship.

Brenner's hands tightened into fists. He lunged forward, his lengthy stride crossing the gap between the bobbling rail and the jetty. He hit the moldered, damp wood with a *thump,* and used the momentum to hasten forward.

Ahead, he spotted the police car that had been sent to pick him up.

In one hand, he held his phone. And the voice coming from it was the main source of his scowl.

"I know, Brenner," Ella was saying over the speaker, her words competing with the howling wind and thrashing surf. "But we need someone to keep an eye on them!"

Brenner didn't stop to give a farewell nod to the coastie waiting in the cutter but made a beeline towards the waiting squad car.

Part of him wanted to ignore Ella. To jump right back in the cutter and rejoin her on the vessel.

"It doesn't feel right leaving you on your own," he said, his voice a growl.

A heavy sigh on the other line. He couldn't see her, but off in the distance, he could just about make out the forms of the coast guard rising up the Jacob's ladder, moving to the deck.

He sighed to himself, muttering under his breath, and wishing he'd put up more of a fight. Ella had been the one who'd suggested they split up. One of them on the boat, searching for the killer or any clues he may have left behind to his whereabouts.

The other heading back to babysit Priscilla Porter and Matthias Baker.

The countdown continued on the website. Brenner occasionally swiped on his phone, away from the call to the website where the killer had posted the digital clock. Only six hours remained until he claimed he was going to kill the sweethearts of Nome.

Princess Priscilla and Homecoming King Mattie Baker.

Brenner scowled, reaching the squad car and snapping. "To the dig site. Go!"

The cop who'd volunteered to drive was a younger man, jumpy and nervous. The poor fellow seemed frightened of Brenner's shadow, but

Brenner didn't have time to spare for frazzled nerves. His mind was on Ella.

The cop was just another reminder of how deep pockets went in Nome. Brenner recognized the guy. Flannel and a beard. The same cop who'd been back at the docks guarding the crabbing pot. Another member of Chief Baker's old high school football team.

Brenner scowled at the side of the nervous officer's bearded face, watching as the man maneuvered down the cold, icy roads, zipping away from the docks and carrying the marshal towards where Priscilla and her husband were currently being safeguarded.

Brenner guessed that half the officers on the force had some sort of personal connection to Chief Baker.

The bearded man in question kept glancing in the rearview mirror, a nervous flicker in his gaze.

Brenner frowned. "What?" he snapped.

"What's that?" the voice on the phone said.

"Not you," Brenner shot back. Then, he added, "I still think this is a stupid idea."

"Brenner you agreed!" Ella snapped.

"That was before the coasties made record time!" he retorted, "And you agreed to stay in the cutter!"

"Yeah, well… This is my job, Brenner," she said, and Ella's tone had gone professional. She didn't get irritated. He couldn't remember the last time he'd seen her lose her temper. Not *really*. But when Ella got professional, cold, he knew she was starting to get irritated.

He sighed and muttered under his breath. "Well, just stay safe then," he said.

His lips tingled as he spoke. Was she punishing him for that stolen kiss? He shook his head. What a stupid move. Kissing a girl in a murder vessel.

Dummy. He thought to himself, scowling, his blue eyes flashing in the rearview mirror.

The cop with the beard was still watching him.

"What?" Brenner snapped, louder.

And this time he hung up on Ella to spare her the desire to react.

Brenner scowled into the rearview mirror at where the man kept watching him.

The cop shifted nervously, swallowed once, and smoothed the front of his beard. The officer said, "Is it true Chief Baker is being targeted?"

Brenner huffed, his bad mood souring his expression further as he stared through the window at the passing terrain surrounding the Nome dockyards.

Most of the vessels had come in from the storm. A few dredges, gold-mining platforms, hadn't even left the harbor. Even the smallest amount of disturbance in the tide would make excavation mining nearly impossible on the open waters.

Brenner had once served as a diver for a dredge-mining operation, but it hadn't suited him.

Mr. Porter, Ella's father, lived under the principle that everyone had a price.

Everyone could be bought.

Brenner frowned as he considered this, watching the docks pass by, his face pressed against the cold glass.

He wasn't sure he shared the sentiment at all.

Gold had always been attractive to Brenner, same as cash, but never all-consuming. He'd seen what obsession could do to a man. His own father was proof of that.

"Yeah," Brenner said. "Step on it, will you?"

The man in the front seat just shook his head, leaning back and letting out a long sigh. "Shit, man. The chief? God damn."

Brenner grunted. The car picked up pace, moving faster through the streets, away from the choppy ocean, away from where Ella was on a boat with three coast guards for backup.

Faster, faster, the vehicle sped forward, racing towards where Priscilla and her husband were being guarded at one of Jameson Porter's dig sites.

The Porter family was always involved somehow.

Ella was still being investigated for the Spring Children debacle. Her friend, the CI, Mortimer Graves had vanished. Priscilla was sniffing around.

And now, on top of it all, someone had stolen something from Jameson Porter's safety deposit box.

And then that same someone, April Renee, had ended up dead at the bottom of the sea with an escaped convict.

How did all the pieces blend together?

Brenner's hand moved to the gun at his hip, testing it, resting on the handle. He shook his head, scowling through the windshield as they veered off in the direction of the mountains, towards the inland mining operation.

Six hours for the killer to fulfill his request.

"We've got like six cops on site," said the officer in the front seat with an important nod. "No way they're getting at Mattie."

"Mattie?" Brenner snorted. "Well... This psycho isn't like other killers. Determined fellow."

"What do you mean?" Another frown in the rearview mirror. Another flicker of unease. Fear?

Brenner didn't like going into combat with a scared wingman. But it couldn't be avoided—still... Ella rarely got scared.

Brenner said, "Bastard melted through a bunker last time to get at Amos Thompson."

"Shit."

"Yeah. Exactly."

The car picked up the pace again, and Brenner's hand never left his weapon, resting against the comforting, cold steel.

Chapter 20

Ella moved through the dark underbelly of the ship a second time, watching where the Coast Guard placed the breaching charges against the two sealed doors in the back of the metallic compartment.

The Coast Guard commander who'd placed the charge held up a hand, and the two others who'd arrived on the second cutter retreated.

Now, the four of them hunkered down in the stairwell, backs braced against the wall.

The commander hesitated, his unshaven jaw looking rugged where it caught the glow from his phone. He said, "Fire-in-the-hole! Anyone in there, back away from the doors, cover your heads and lay on the ground! Take cover! Hear me?"

No response.

"Last chance!" he shouted, his voice echoing in the metallic underbelly of the ship. "Open the door and we can avoid this!"

Silence met him, carried by a faint echoing sound.

The commander shrugged, glancing at Ella, and she gave the nod. There was a click on his phone, a few seconds.

And then...

Boom!

An echoing blast filled the underbelly of the ship. A flash of orange light reflected off the floor beyond the stairwell. Ella's back pressed to the cold wall of the stairwell, her feet braced on the metallic steps as a wave of warmth gusted towards her.

The doors were blasted open, metal flying in all directions, and the corridor beyond was filled with smoke and dust.

The commander and the two Coast Guard officers moved in, Ella following, her Glock drawn, her eyes scanning the darkness beyond the smoke.

The metal steps and walls of the corridor were dented and twisted, the metal ripped and torn, and the room beyond the two doors was filled with the smell of gasoline and the smoldering remains of a broken generator.

The commander and the two officers moved around the broken generator, and Ella followed, her gun raised, her eyes scanning the darkness.

And then she saw something.

A figure, slumped in the corner, a small figure in a hoodie and jeans.

Ella and the coast guard officers moved closer, and the figure shifted, moaning softly.

It was Hannah Bartlow.

The young woman was soaked, her eyes unfocused and her breathing ragged. She was barely conscious, but alive.

Ella stared, stunned, frozen amidst a haze of lingering smoke and the scent of spent explosives.

She blinked, certain she was seeing things.

But Hannah, the woman who she'd seen in the cage, thrown into the ocean, was sitting there, in a puddle of sea water, barely conscious.

Her eyes flickered, her hands splayed on the ground at either side of her like limp, dead fish.

The commander stooped and checked her vitals, his face grim. He said, "We need to get her out of here. Now."

Ella nodded, her eyes still on Hannah. She said, "Take her."

The coast guard officers moved in, lifting the woman from the ground with gentle care, and Ella stepped back, her mind buzzing.

What had happened? How had Hannah made it here?

The questions raced through her mind, but the answers were nowhere to be found.

For now, all that mattered was that she was safe.

Ella watched as the officers moved Hannah up the stairs, her eyes lingering on the broken figure.

She'd been through so much.

But she was alive. Ella needed to know what had happened, and part of her almost moved after the woman to try and ask questions.

She watched as two of the coast guard disappeared, the woman carried between them, hurrying up the steps. She could already hear the buzz of a radio as they called for paramedics.

But Ella caught herself, stopping and turning back out of the generator room to face the *second* door that had been blasted.

She still had to search the ship.

There was still a killer to catch down here.

She moved through the mangled mess of metal of the second door, shouldering through, turning sideways to avoid a jutting flap of sharp steel.

Behind her, she heard the commander speaking into his radio, issuing rapid instructions.

She paused, peering into the dark ahead of her, raising her toolbelt flashlight to shine it through the dim space.

This area was much larger than the generator room, and debris littered the floor at her feet, scattered across the ground.

What had happened here?

She moved further in, her flashlight beam sweeping across the walls, the floor, and then she saw it.

A large metal safe, the kind used in a bank.

Ella's breath caught, her heart racing.

April Renee had stolen something from Jameson Porter's safety deposit box.

She moved closer, her eyes scanning the safe, searching for a way to open it.

She found the keypad and a small card scanner.

Ella raised her weapon, pointing it at the keypad. She glanced around the dark, expansive space. The sound of the commander's voice could still be heard through the open and mangled door.

She paused, raised her gun and fired twice.

The lock on the safe shattered, sparking.

She stepped forward, reaching down and turning the handle. The safe opened with a *click*.

She pulled on the door, frowning, staring into the safe.

What was going on?

How was everything connected?

She shivered, trying to make sense of it all but failing.

As she bent double, she felt suddenly exposed, standing by a crate as large as she was, facing old, metal shelves laden with thick piping and discarded tools. For a moment, in the dark, she felt as if she were being watched.

She frowned, her gaze sweeping across the space.

She shivered briefly, still staring.

Her breath came out in a slow gust as she straightened, peering into the dark, the safe open at her feet, but her eyes now moving along the shelves, searching for movement.

"Hello?" she called out. "Hello? Who's there?"

No reply.

No response.

The sound of the commander's voice had faded now. She was left in the quiet. Alone in the dark.

She turned back to glance towards the open, shattered door, but she spotted something in the safe as she moved, and she paused, turning again.

Her skin prickled.

She reached out, hesitantly, extending her fingers towards the safe with caution.

Inside were two items, a metal box and a small, leatherbound book.

Ella opened the metal box first. A flash drive. She stared at it, frowning.

Was this the same item that had been taken from her father's security deposit box?

She then looked at the leatherbound book, opening it.

She immediately felt a flicker of excitement.

Her father's handwriting.

She instantly recognized the cramped, doctor-style cursive. Nearly illegible.

But then she read the names... dates... and the list of items on each page.

Names like: *Dr. Casper Manchin. Affair. Cocaine.*

Or something like, *Chief Matthias Baker. Pornography. Alcohol.*

Aspen Carmichael. Cigarettes. Gossip.

The list went on and on. Ella stared, flipping one page to the other. She froze as she read. *Brenner Gunn. Alcohol. PTSD.*

It took a second for it to dawn on her. But then she let out a little gasp. She stared at the small, leather-bound book in her hand and closed it instantly. Her eyes darted to the flash drive.

Evidence, undoubtedly.

This drive, she realized, was a book of leverage. Blackmail her father accumulated to use on everyone in Nome. Anyone he needed to push one way or another.

And he had stored it with the owner of a news agency. Had given Carmichael a key...

Because Carmichael was also on the hook. But on top of it... because if anyone ever came after Jameson Porter, if they fought back, then a news agent could leak all the sordid information to the press.

Ella stared, her heart in her throat.

She swallowed briefly, feeling a cold chill down her spine.

The book quivered in her hands, and she nearly dropped it.

It felt dirty. Gross.

She stared at the item and resisted the urge to sprint back up the stairs and throw it overboard.

There could be evidence within.

Now... someone had killed April Renee over recovering this book.

Was it because they were ashamed of what was in it? So why was the book still intact? Why hadn't it been destroyed?

Likely it wasn't the only copy. Had her father sent a copy to Amos Thompson?

A criminal who'd set up shop in Nome. Perhaps her father had his hooks in the man as well.

What about Hannah, though?

The survivor?

Ella frowned, listening to the rocking sway of the ocean outside the metallic walls.

Clang.

She turned sharply, her heart leaping into her throat. She shoved the book and the flash drive into her pocket, whirling around.

She stared into the dark, her gaze scanning the wide, open space, like that of a cargo hold or perhaps a low-ceilinged warehouse.

She took a few steps forward, her flashlight beam sweeping back and forth, her gun drawn.

She heard something.

The sound of breathing.

She froze, staring into the dark.

Her heart was pounding in her chest, her breath coming in short, shallow bursts.

She heard it again.

A low, shuffling sound.

Her heart stopped.

Slowly, she crept forward, her gun raised and ready.

She saw a faint glimmer of light ahead and her throat tightened. She didn't speak, didn't move, her gun clutched tightly now.

Behind one of the shelves...

Someone was here.

Ella moved in cautiously. Had Amos survived as well? What was going on here?

She moved forward now, gun in hand, her fingers tight, her palm sweaty, trembling.

She stepped around the edge of the shelving, brushing up near a cardboard box filled with wooden blocks and shims. Her light and weapon swept towards the space.

Nothing.

She stared into the dark.

No movement, no motion.

An empty aisle leading to a dusty, rusted wall.

She'd heard breathing, hadn't she?

She frowned, cautiously stepping down the aisle.

She heard the faintest of grunts and whirled around.

She spotted an opening in the aisle, under one of the metal shelves. Just large enough for someone to crawl through.

And now, the sound had come from *outside* the room.

Ella cursed, breaking into a sprint, her mind racing, panic flaring.

She lurched out to where the coast guard had been.

And she stumbled to a halt, spotting where he now lay, a knife buried in his neck. He lay in a pool of blood, motionless, clearly attacked from behind.

Ella's heart leapt in her throat. She sprinted towards the Coast Guard commander's side, avoiding the blood.

She knelt beside him, checking his pulse.

Nothing.

He was dead.

Ella's jaw tightened. She had to find out who had done this.

She scrambled to her feet, scanning the room, her gun raised.

Whoever had done this was still here.

The killer was here with her, in the dark, on the ship.

She glanced towards the stairwell. A slick stain of blood on one step.

A footprint?

She cursed and broke into a sprint towards the stairs.

Hannah and the two other coasties were still on deck. They wouldn't know the killer was coming.

And as she reached the stairs, she glanced back.

The gun from the commander's holster was missing.

The killer was on the ship, armed.

She broke into a dead sprint, taking the stairs with clanging steps.

Chapter 21

Brenner was frowning, shaking his head as he pushed out of the back of the vehicle, glancing in the direction of the inland mining operation.

"What's the matter?" Officer Taylor asked.

Brenner hadn't asked for the man's name, but the bearded cop had volunteered it. A virtual chatterbox, this guy, and Brenner was growing tired of it.

Still, Brenner just shook his head, staring towards the metal mesh fence circling the dig site. Brenner scratched at his chin, pausing and glancing back towards the squad car.

Three other squad cars were parked in the front lot.

Through the fence, he spotted a small, corrugated trailer where two police were standing out front, hands on their weapons.

Another two cops were positioned by a mechanic shed, behind the office building.

In the distance, Brenner spotted tall mountains of dirt. The wash plant for the mine site was still running, and dirt and debris was sent up the conveyor belt to be sprayed, shaken and then sifted.

A digger was depositing sediment into a rock truck, and a mechanic was tending to one of the water pumps, trying to dislodge some chunks of ice from within an O-ring.

Brenner took it all in quickly, looking for threats, for potential obstacles and for any tactical information.

As a sniper, he'd been trained to take in a scene within seconds.

Now, though, he was shaking his head. "Something's off," he said to Officer Taylor.

The cop had fallen into step at Brenner's side. The two of them moved through the open chain link fence towards the trailer where the two cops were standing sentry.

A Range Rover in the parking lot suggested Priscilla and her husband were still here as well.

"What's off?" Taylor said conversationally, his gloved hands hooked through his belt, below the fluff of his winter coat.

Brenner just shook his head.

"One guy... one guy broke through a window, grabbed Amos? One guy was able to pull him out?"

"How's that?" said the cop, conversationally.

Brenner paused, his breath foggy in front of his face, his cheeks tingling from the cold. He adjusted his gloves on his hands, then reached into his pocket, pulling out his phone.

A missed call from Ella.

He frowned, held up a finger, and called back.

The trailer door opened as he stood twenty paces away, between the entrance to the dig site and the office trailer.

Through the door, he spotted Priscilla Porter frowning out at him, one hand on her hip.

It was always jarring to spend time with Ella and then to see Cilla. It gave him whiplash.

The two looked so similar, but the expressions they wore, the auras they projected, were so different.

One of them cold, cruel and defiant. The other guarded, considerate and quiet.

Both of them with wills of steel, though.

Both of them stubborn to their core, in their own ways.

Brenner looked away from where Cilla stood in the doorway, his phone ringing.

Ella didn't pick up.

He frowned, tapping his foot against the dusty ground, dislodging small rocks from the trail where they had apparently tumbled from the back of rock trucks.

"Come on, Ella," he muttered. "Pick up."

"I don't get it," Taylor was saying, shaking his head and still chattering away as he'd done on the drive over. "What do you mean one guy got Amos?"

"I mean," Brenner said, gruff, still waiting for his phone to connect, "That it wasn't a one-man job. I wasn't paying close enough attention..." He paused, then shook his head. "Actually, I wasn't paying *broad* enough attention. I missed the forest for the trees."

"What?"

This, Brenner decided, was Officer Taylor's favorite word. But Ella wasn't picking up, and now Brenner's anxiety spiked.

He cursed and tried again.

Priscilla was calling out to him now, waving a hand, her voice piercing like a queen commanding a subject.

Brenner scowled, pacing back and forth, but the call still didn't connect.

His mind was racing. Out loud, he muttered, "What if there's a second?"

"How's that?" whispered the officer.

"A second killer," Brenner said, going still, cold and motionless. "It would explain a lot. How the killer was able to take Hannah and Amos. How the killer was able to get away with four other murders. Set up a computer. Besides... someone is holding the camera..." Brenner considered this now. There had been only the faintest of motion with the camera in the videos.

He'd thought the lens on a tripod had been jarred.

But by whom?

Someone had bumped it.

A second person.

Someone else had been in the room when the killer had filmed his mocking videos.

Brenner felt a shiver now, goosebumps spreading across his arms.

"Shit," he muttered, turning sharply and beginning to hasten back towards the car.

"Brenner!" Priscilla called out.

But he was moving quickly now, racing towards the squad car. "Two killers. Ella was trapped on that ship with *two* killers."

He'd been an idiot. He'd come to protect Cilla because Ella had asked him to.

But he never should have left.

He never should have...

Gunshots resounded. Someone screamed. Brenner blinked a couple of times, pausing, confused briefly.

And then the pain flared through his back. He'd been shot.

He stumbled, striking the ground.

As he turned, he spotted the two cops by the door scrambling for their weapons.

But Officer Taylor, the same cop who'd been there when they'd found the body of his escaped convict, was whirling around, gun raised.

Two more blasts.

The first cop hit the ground, dead, blood speckling the corrugated wall behind him.

Officer Taylor was no longer trembling, no longer fragile and frazzled.

Instead, he wore a grim expression, his eyes narrowed into slits.

Two more shots as the final cop tried to pull his gun.

Too late.

Both guards by the door lay dead on the ground in pools of red. And Taylor broke into a sprint towards the door.

Brenner's vision swam as he stared. He could feel his own blood pooling beneath him.

The last glimpse he had before darkness came was of Priscilla shouting something, slamming the door.

Then two bullet holes appeared in the metal, directly where Priscilla had been standing.

Officer Taylor unloaded on the trailer, blasting it to bits.

Brenner tried to shout a warning.

The other cops by the machine shop were nowhere to be seen. In on it? Slow?

Shot?

Brenner's mind was slowing now. He couldn't quite keep his eyes open.

Darkness closed in. Spots at first, but the spots widened.

He blinked a few times and let out a faint groan...

And then he fell unconscious, laying in the dirt, bleeding.

Chapter 22

A killer lurked somewhere in the dark, and Ella had lost track of him.

She moved slowly, up the metal steps, listening as the rusted surface groaned underfoot.

She paused, standing at the top of a stairwell, one hand gripping her weapon, the other trailing against the wall to keep her bearings.

No flashlight—she hadn't wanted the killer to see her coming.

Behind her, at the base of the stairs, she could just glimpse the corner of a rapidly spreading pool of blood where the Coast Guard commander lay motionless.

Her breath came slowly, and she trembled. Her heart skipped a beat and sweat prickled on her brow.

Ahead of her, a twenty-yard hallway led through the accommodations where fishermen would sleep during the nights, under the wheelhouse, where the captain would normally reside.

She hesitated, listening intently.

No sound.

Her fingers itched where they touched against the rough walls.

Somewhere, the two other coast guards had taken Hannah Bartlow to their cutter.

But the killer was armed, having stolen the murdered man's gun.

Ella cursed. She couldn't linger.

She summoned courage and bolted from the cover of the stairwell, emerging in the hallway, all too aware that any of the four closed doorways of the crew quarters could suddenly slam open, allowing for an ambush.

But gunshots never came.

She raced forward, up the hall, pausing at each door and peering in. She moved from one room to the next, scanning them one at a time, her nerves slowly steadying as adrenaline pumped, as she pushed aside fear and focused on the task at hand.

She could feel her body tensing, her brow furrowing, her eyes attentive and alert.

She wondered where Brenner was, but then pushed this thought aside.

The first room on her left was clear, an empty space with a cot in one corner sans a mat and stains on the ground that looked like bleach.

She moved to the next room, shouldering it open slowly. The door creaked.

The room was empty, save for a single chair and a wardrobe.

She pushed back the wardrobe, her hands trembling.

Behind it, nothing.

She moved on, checking each room until she was standing at the last one.

This one was different.

The door was ajar, and a strange light shone from within.

She stepped forward, peering cautiously through the crack.

The room had been transformed.

On the bed was a lump, under a blanket. Ella stared, her eyes wide.

Her stomach tightened and she stepped back, her breath quickening.

The lump under the blanket looked to be the size of a body... the killer?

She stood still, listening.

Silence.

She steeled her nerves and stepped forward, pushing the door open with a loud creak.

The figure on the bed didn't move. She thought she glimpsed a tuft of hair.

Ella's heart raced, and she felt a chill run down her spine.

She approached cautiously, gun clutched in one hand, holding it steady.

"Hands where I can see them," she said slowly, her voice like iron. She surprised herself with how harsh her tone was.

In a way, it reminded her of her father.

She frowned, troubled by this thought. But she stepped forward again, now standing next to the bed.

She remained far enough away to avoid the killer if he lunged.

But the figure on the bed looked to be facing the wall. No sign of a gun.

Was this the man who'd stabbed the coast guard?

She reached out, hesitantly, pausing only briefly.

The hair color looked vaguely familiar. Dark and wavy... Long, too.

Ella stared, frozen in place. And then she reached out, snatching at the blanket and pulling it aside like a magician's flourish.

And then she gasped.

The figure on the bed was unconscious. Her arms bound in front of her. Her legs bound too.

She was bleeding from a gash in her forehead.

For a moment, Ella thought for certain the woman was dead.

But then she let out a faint groan, moving slowly. The woman's eyes fluttered, and Ella realized the muffled sounds came from her breathing, as she was gagged.

Most astounding of all... Ella recognized the bound woman.

April Renee.

"You're supposed to be dead..." Ella murmured to herself before she could help it.

The shock sent jolts of cold along her arms, her fingers feeling as if they were fizzing.

She stared at the beautiful woman who'd been identified by dental records as the victim in the first crab pot.

But the dental records had clearly been faked.

The skeleton found in the metal cage the week before belonged to some other poor victim.

This, undoubtedly, was the face of April Renee.

Even with the grime and the dirt and the blood from the wound, Ella could discern the jaw-dropping beauty of the news anchor.

The woman who'd stolen from her father's safety deposit box.

She was still alive.

For a moment, Ella just stared, stunned, and then she surged forward, trying to tug at the ropes binding the woman's hands.

"You're going to be okay!" Ella said quickly, tugging at the ropes.

The woman's eyes were fluttering now, and she looked incoherent. She was gasping desperately, moaning as she did. Her eyes widened in fright as Ella reached out but then softened as Ella aimed her gun in a different direction.

"My name is Agent Porter. I'm with the FBI. You're safe. Can you tell me who did this?"

Suddenly, Ella thought she heard a creaking sound above from the wheelhouse, the captain's quarters.

She froze, staring up at the metal ceiling.

The creaking sound stopped.

But April's eyes had flared in a panic, and she shrunk back, leaning against the wall, gasping desperately.

Ella checked the hall, making sure the killer wasn't sneaking up on her, and then she hastened back to the woman on the bed, quickly struggling to untie the knots.

As Ella worked, murmuring soothingly, her mind flitted to Hannah Bartlow and the coast guard. Somehow Hannah had also survived.

Ella hadn't heard gunshots yet, which meant for the moment Hannah and the officers were safe.

But Ella had to hurry.

She managed to ungag the woman first and then began untying the woman's wrists.

The ropes were taut and knotted multiple times.

It took Ella several tense and frustrating minutes to undo the knots, but finally, the ropes fell away. She helped the woman sit up, checking her for any other injuries. Once she'd determined the only wound was the superficial one on the head, Ella looked April in the eyes.

"Who did this to you?" Ella asked again, her voice low and urgent.

April was struggling to breathe, her long-lashed eyes darting around the room in fear. "He... he said he was going to kill me," she whispered, her voice hoarse. "He said I knew too much."

Ella frowned. "Who said? Who is he?"

April shook her head, her eyes pleading. "I don't know his name. He... he wore a mask. He was always in the shadows. He was always watching me."

Ella's heart raced.

"He killed the coast guard, but spared you..." Ella said, more to herself than to April.

April nodded, her eyes wide with fear. "He... he said he was going to kill me, too. He said I knew too much about... about what happened on that boat."

Ella frowned. "What boat?"

April shook her head, her eyes closing as if in pain. "I don't remember. It's all a blur. He... he drugged me. I woke up on that boat, and... and there was blood everywhere. I... I tried to run, but he caught me. He... he said he was going to make me pay for what I saw."

Ella's mind raced, trying to piece it all together. She was missing something. That much was clear. Ella helped April sit up, and the woman looked at her with a mix of fear and gratitude.

"Thank you," she said weakly.

Ella nodded, her eyes scanning over her shoulder, back towards the hall once more, for any sign of the killer. She could hear creaks once more now, coming from the direction of the wheelhouse, an eerie, echoing groan of metal above her.

Footsteps?

Too heavy... Something else?

"What is that?" April whispered, her voice shaking.

Ella just shook her head, holding a finger to her lips. So many of Ella's own questions whirred through her head. Questions she wanted to ask April, but now wasn't the time.

The killer was still out there.

"We have to go," she said, helping April to her feet. "Can you walk?"

April nodded, and they began making their way down the hallway. Ella kept her gun trained on the door to the wheelhouse, at the top of a small flight of stairs, ready for the killer to make an appearance.

But as they neared the end of the hallway, the door remained shut. Ella froze in place, desperately trying to piece it all together.

She was missing something.

"Can you tell me what he looked like?" she whispered to April, the two of them pausing at the exit to the deck.

A gust of breeze swept through the open metal door.

The cold swelled over Ella's skin, raising goosebumps.

She strained to listen to the distant sounds, over the sea, over the wind.

But no gunshots.

No movement.

Even the creaking from above had faded.

April just shook her head. "He was small," she whispered. "But... but there were two of them!"

Ella stared.

"Two?"

"Yeah," April moaned. "I think... I think one of them was a cop."

This sent chills along Ella's hands. "Are you sure?" she said sharply. "A cop?"

Her mind immediately flashed to Brenner.

More fear settled in her. But again, she had to tackle problems one at a time. Getting herself and April shot wasn't going to help Brenner.

But the idea of *two* shooters lurking on the boat was hardly a comforting one.

"We need to get out of here," Ella said, taking April's arm and pulling her towards the door to the deck. "The Coast Guard is anchored against the ship, but we need to get out of here before we're seen."

April nodded slowly but limped as she did. She looked reluctant to take the lead and gestured for Ella to move ahead of her, fear in the woman's eyes.

Ella didn't blame her. She wasn't sure what had happened to April, nor why the killer had spared her life or gone to the trouble of faking the woman's dental records, but clearly April was in over her head.

Ella stepped forward, taking the lead, using her own body as a protective shield for the beautiful woman.

She moved onto the deck of the crabbing vessel.

The salty sea air hit her nostrils, and Ella felt a sense of relief at being out in the open. The endless stretch of water lay before her, visible through the gaps in the encircling rail of rust, with the emerging moon casting a silver sheen over the waves. Evening had come now, and she scanned the deck, looking for any signs of danger. The ropes creaked against the mast, and the water lapped against the sides of the boat, creating a soothing rhythm. But the peace was short-lived.

Ella heard a faint whisper, like someone talking nearby. She tightened her grip on her gun and signaled for April to stay low. They made their way towards the edge of the boat, trying to stay hidden from view. Ella peeked around the corner and saw two figures standing by the railings. One of them was tall, with broad shoulders and a cap pulled down over his face. The other was shorter, with a lean build.

Both of them were trying to help a woman over the railing, discussing, in hushed voices, the best way to navigate the Jacob's ladder to reach the boat below.

Ella felt a flicker of relief.

She relaxed as she recognized the coast guard, but then she remembered April's warning that one of the killers was potentially a cop.

Ella stepped out, moving towards the guards, her gun still in hand but pointed at the ground.

The two men glanced over at her, and one of them frowned.

The stocky one said, "Where's Greg?"

Ella hesitated, glancing back towards where April was moving slowly, wincing as she gingerly limped along the deck.

Ella began to return to help the woman and didn't answer the question.

She couldn't bring herself to.

"Hey," said the coastie once more. "Where's Greg?"

Ella shook her head. "Dead," she said.

The two men stared at her.

Hannah Bartlow was pale-faced, wrapped in a warm blanket, sitting on the deck between them by the ladder.

Now, though, the coast guards who'd had hands on Hannah's shoulders went stiff.

"What was that?" said the stocky man, his face like a mask.

"Dead," Ella said simply, her voice strained. "The killer is still on the ship."

"Greg's dead?" said the stocky man. "Hell no," he snapped, his teeth flashing in the moon, setting out like a crescent in his dark features.

He stomped forward now, approaching her as if determined to race past her and check for himself.

The second coast guard tried to reach out and grab at his companion but missed.

Ella was shaking her head. "I'm so sorry!"

"He wouldn't just die!" snapped the coastie. "Greg wouldn't go down without a fight!"

Ella winced, shaking her head.

"Hang on, Marcus!" snapped the other coastie. "You're going to get yourself killed. Stay here!"

The squat man stumbled to a stop, and Ella detected tears in his eyes.

Her heart panged.

But something was gnawing at her.

Something the coastie had said.

Greg wouldn't go down without a fight...

And what if he hadn't?

What if he had put up a fight then been stabbed?

Would he have injured the killer?

She remembered seeing blood on the stairs. She hesitated only briefly, her heart in her throat. Two killers.

April Renee was alive.

How?

Someone had faked her dental records...

Who would want to do that?

The killer?

Why?

Would he have had the access?

Maybe... but what about someone at a news agency? Someone with connections like Carmichael? Someone whose features were so attractive that most men would stumble over themselves trying to get the person's approval.

Beauty was a type of superpower after all.

Ella hesitated only briefly.

Paused...

The knot on the ropes had been facing the woman... Not facing Ella... Facing April.

The knots hadn't been facing the right direction... Almost as if...

As if April had tied herself up.

And the wound on her head?

Greg wouldn't have gone down without a fight. And he hadn't.

Ella spun around, prickles erupting across her skin, her own gun rising, snapping to attention and pointing at April Renee's face.

"Don't move!" Ella snapped, her voice harsh. "Don't you dare move!"

She wasn't sure what she'd been hearing above her in the captain's wheelhouse, but now, around her, she could hear the similar creak and groan of metal.

Everywhere. The wind and the waves, the rocking of the vessel being affected by the motion of the ocean.

The sounds had been a distraction.

The real threat was staring right at her. A perfectly symmetrical face forming a wide-eyed look of surprise and innocence.

But Ella trusted her instincts.

She'd had one of the best records apprehending serial killers before she'd been exiled to Nome.

She wasn't afraid of risk.

And now, she pointed her gun at the woman with the injured head.

"The knots were facing the wrong direction," she said simply. "And that wound is fresh."

April Renee didn't move, frozen in place. Confusion reigned, and the coast guards were both calling out to her, though she wasn't listening to their placations.

The moon shone down like a spotlight as night continued to intrude.

And Ella's hands were as steady as a rock in the surf.

"I said don't move!" she snapped.

April's hand had twitched towards the back of her waistband.

And a strange glint had appeared in the woman's eyes.

Chapter 23

Brenner groaned, his eyes fluttering as he drifted in and out of consciousness.

He was laying on the ground, under the watchful moon as flecks of snow fell onto his nose.

He nearly sneezed, but then a jolt of pain flared through his right shoulder.

It was wet.

Blood, he realized.

His own damn blood.

He groaned, gritting his teeth.

His consciousness was going to fade again, and he could feel his mind trying to retreat into the safety of sleep. But he couldn't let that happen.

Ella was in danger.

Cilla was in danger.

Brenner groaned and then, gritting his teeth, he slammed his right shoulder against the ground.

Pain flared through him.

A sharp, biting, gnawing pain that ripped a gasp from his lungs. He groaned as small bits of gravel from the ground and discarded rock truck debris bit into the gunshot wound in his back. His shoulder was on fire.

But it roused him, like smelling salts.

He groaned, sitting up slowly. He could feel the blood pouring down his shoulder, staining his back. The warmth swaddled him, almost like a blanket in the cold dig site.

He could hear gunshots in the distance and blinked as he tried to adjust his vision.

He didn't have time to be slow about it.

"Come on, asshole," he muttered to himself.

Brenner pushed to his feet, clenched teeth biting back a gasp.

Agony lanced through his form, but it only roused him to further consciousness.

Now, black spots across his vision faded. The pain was so intense, it was as if it wouldn't *let* him fall asleep.

But he was losing a lot of blood.

He could feel it dripping down his back.

He reached up, testing at his shoulder in the front.

No exit wound.

The bullet was still in there.

In a way, this was favorable given the circumstances.

Only one hole to plug.

He thought dispassionately about his options as he gave a quick glance to survey the dig site.

Bullet holes littered the front of the trailer where Cilla and her husband had sheltered.

But the door was now off the hinges.

The gunshots were coming from further in the dig site, beyond a large pile of tailings—a virtual mountain of dust and rock and discarded debris.

The sounds were nearly a half mile away, but he could occasionally spot a muzzle flare, his trained eyes picking them out amidst the rock trucks parked on the opposite side of the dig site.

He groaned and grit his teeth, but knew he had to stop the bleeding.

And so he reached up, tearing a piece of fabric off the base of his shirt, using a utility knife from his pocket to complete the motion.

He leaned forward as he worked, helping to redirect the blood flow.

He had to move fast.

"Come on, asshole," he repeated.

Not exactly the most inspiring mantra.

But it had worked in the past. He could remember more than one stake-out, in the cold, or the blaring heat where he'd been forced to watch some target for days before taking a shot.

'Come on, asshole' had kept him going.

It was also, growing up, his father's favorite term for Brenner.

Brenner scowled, gripping the newly ripped piece of fabric, rolling it into a ball, and then, wincing, he reached back towards his shoulder.

The gunshots continued in the distance.

He let out a hiss as he wadded the fabric into the wound. He groaned as he did it, hot needles stabbing through his back, but once he'd finished, he pulled blood-slicked fingers away, removed his belt, and lashed it over his shoulder like a bandolier.

He tightened the belt as much as he could, pulling it taught and using it to put pressure on the wound.

Gunshot wounds always required more pressure than someone expected, enough to indent the skin.

He let out another gasp of pain but was now beginning to get pissed off at himself.

"Pansy. Wuss. Dumbass," he muttered to himself. "Don't be a bitch." He slapped his own face, trying to shock himself.

The tight wrap around his shoulder restricted the movement of his right arm.

His shooting hand.

He glanced at the ground, looking desperately for his gun, and then he spotted it, laying in a pool of his own blood.

He cursed, bent, snatched it in his left hand, and then began to move.

It wasn't quite a jog, but more of a stumbling-lurching motion.

Still, he made his way past the bullet-riddled trailer in the direction of the mountain of tailings half a mile away.

He glanced into the trailer as he passed. A desk had been knocked over, also splintered with bullets.

He frowned.

The dirty cop had shot him... but there were too many bullets to have come from only one gun.

Were there others involved?

Cilla and Chief Baker had obviously fired back.

Were they still alive?

No bodies in the trailer that he could see. A blood stain on the door.

He grit his teeth, flustered, and kept moving. The gunshots continued to resound ahead.

He spotted someone hunkered down, a shadowy figure, behind one of the rock trucks.

He scowled, moving towards them, his gun clutched in his left hand. But he couldn't make out the figure from this distance.

Friend or foe?

Pain flared, distracting him again, but he kept pushing forward with his strange, stilted gait.

As Brenner approached the pile of tailings, he could hear voices shouting over the sound of gunfire. He crouched down behind a boulder, panting with exertion and pain. He had to catch his breath and assess the situation. The dig site was a warzone, with bullets flying from all directions. Brenner could see men in black tactical gear moving through the piles of dirt and rock, firing their weapons at someone who'd taken shelter in the machine shed. Three of them surged forward.

Brenner stared, eyes wide.

He didn't recognize those men.

Not SWAT.

Not cops.

Mercenaries?

Gun thugs?

He didn't know. What was going on here?

It was chaos, and Brenner knew he had to act fast if he wanted to survive. He focused on his breathing, trying to slow his heart rate and clear his head. He needed to discern friend from foe.

The three men with the tactical outfits joined the hunched figure behind the rock truck and the four of them disappeared from sight, moving around the truck to try and circle the warehouse-shaped machine shed.

Someone in the second floor of the shed ducked behind a window, their silhouette thin and small. He spotted blonde hair.

Cilla?

Shit.

She was in trouble. Where was Baker?

He could see a group of workers huddled behind a bulldozer, taking cover from the gunfire. They were unarmed and vulnerable. Brenner knew he had to do something to help them. He took a deep breath and pushed himself up from behind the boulder, raising his gun and firing at the attackers. His right arm was weak and unsteady, but he managed to hit one of the men in the leg as he circled the shed, causing him to stumble forwards with a shout. The workers by the bulldozer looked over at Brenner in surprise, and he gestured towards them, mouthing the words "get out of here."

He gestured for them to retreat from the direction they'd come.

"It's clear!" he said hurriedly. "Go!"

And then he moved forward.

The workers fled past him, and he sheltered behind the dozer now, going still, breathing heavily.

He could hear shouting as the gunmen realized someone was flanking them from behind.

A helmeted head poked from behind the edge of the warehouse, aiming and firing at Brenner.

Sparks flew off the yellowed metal of the dozer.

Brenner ducked. His back ached, and blood streaked above him. He had to readjust the tight belt on his right shoulder, but once he did, he released a pent-up breath.

The workers had now fled past the trailer, kicking up dust in their wake.

They were safe, for now.

But the same couldn't be said for whoever was in the machine shed.

If it was Cilla, she was being flanked.

Two of the gunmen had veered off, though. Both of them wearing black tactical gear, both of them moving towards where Brenner crouched, keeping low, moving from rock pile to rock pile for cover.

He was bleeding, dazed, exhausted, and shooting with his left hand.

Not to mention, there were four gunmen and only one of him.

He didn't know *what* was going on here.

But he knew he had to do something about it.

And staying still would get him killed.

The attackers were getting closer, and Brenner could see their faces under their dark helmets and above their bulletproof vests.

He recognized one of them. The man had a scar above his eyebrow and a cruel smirk on his lips. It was the same man who had been sitting at the bar back at the Three Dwarves.

Organized crime.

Some of Amos Thompson's goons. What was going on here?

Brenner didn't know. Clearly, this wasn't just a serial killer case.

Something else was going on here.

Something dark.

As the two gunmen hastened forward, though, trying to flank him, Brenner felt a surge of anger rise up within him, and he took a deep breath, steadying his aim with his left hand.

He aimed for the scar-faced man. A narrow shot.

An impossible shot on the move, left-handed, for most.

But Brenner wasn't most.

He emerged from behind his cover, moving swiftly, his arm like a whip.

He fired off a shot, hitting the oncoming man in the shoulder, causing him to stumble backward with a curse. The other attacker turned towards Brenner, aiming his gun in his direction. Brenner gritted his teeth, taking aim once more.

But before he could fire, a sudden explosion rocked the ground beneath them, causing both Brenner and the attacker to lose their footing. Brenner fell backward, hitting his head on a rock and blacking out for a brief moment. When he came to, he saw that the attacker had disappeared, and a thick cloud of smoke was rising up from the direction of the machine shed.

He blinked, his ears ringing, trying to figure out what had happened.

He glimpsed Priscilla standing in the window, cursing and hefting something in one hand.

A grenade.

A *second* grenade.

The evidence of the first was the ringing in Brenner's ears, the cloud of smoke and the shrapnel *tinking* against the diggers around them.

Brenner gaped at where Priscilla flashed her middle finger through the window in his direction, and then turned, aiming her second grenade around the side of the warehouse.

She flung the device.

A few seconds.

Then another *boom!*

Just like Cilla, he thought. Bringing an incendiary device to a gunfight.

Brenner scrambled to his feet, his head spinning. He could hear shouting and footsteps approaching from around the side of the warehouse.

The final two gunmen having been smoked out by the explosive. He knew he had to get to cover and fast.

He could hear the men cursing.

And then he spotted the bearded asshole who'd shot him.

The cop emerged, stumbling.

And Brenner discarded all thoughts of running for cover.

Instead, he stood his ground.

Ears still ringing, smoke rising around him.

His arm in a makeshift sling. His gun in his offhand, standing over the body of a man he'd shot.

He waited, patiently, not moving an inch.

He waited until the two gunmen fully emerged, standing like a statue.

They'd been looking for motion, like most men in combat, searching for movement rather than stationary targets.

And so when Brenner's hand whipped up again, they both shouted in unison, raising their arms as well, sighting in on him.

Two against one.

But Brenner had always been fast.

It wasn't a fair fight.

He fired twice.

Caught one between the eyes. A perfect shot.

The bearded asshole got two to the chest.

Both collapsed within a split-second of each other, like marionettes with snipped strings.

He let out a long breath, staring at the dead men.

The gunshots faded around him.

The sounds of battle disappeared.

He stood alone, out in the open, staring at three men he'd shot dead.

His vision was swimming again.

He spotted Cilla in the window, looking down at him, imperious as ever.

In a way, she'd always looked down on him.

No...

No, he thought to himself.

Not always.

There was a time when...

But then Cilla let out a little breath, and she collapsed, clutching at her ribs, disappearing from sight in the window.

His eyes widened in horror.

Brenner started to run, his left arm clutching his wounded right shoulder. The pain was excruciating, but he forced himself to keep moving, his heart pounding in his chest. He didn't know who to trust, or what was really going on here. But he knew one thing for sure—he had to survive.

Cilla needed him.

Ella was in danger.

He broke into a dead sprint, agony lancing through him at every motion, but he didn't stop. He couldn't.

Chapter 24

Ella gripped her gun, pointing it at April Renee, and it was as if time slowed.

The two women's eyes locked, and they both tensed.

Ella didn't blink.

She had to be right... Didn't she?

April stammered, her eyes widening, her voice shaking with fear. "P-please," she whimpered. "Please!"

"It's just a game. It all started in love," Ella said softly. "A beautiful woman like you... it's easy to get people to fall in love, isn't it?"

April's hand still hovered at her waist, hidden behind her hip as if she were scratching at her lower back.

Or reaching for a weapon.

The weapon she'd taken from the man she'd killed.

How could someone in this decaying, echoing, bucket of rust sneak up on a trained coast guardsman in the dark without being spotted?

Close enough to stab them?

A pretty, frail young woman?

That might be enough.

"You tied the ropes yourself," Ella said softly. "And then you hid on the bed, knowing we'd find you..."

"Wh-what are you talking about?" she said, her voice trembling.

"You can cut the act. Your dental records were changed. Only one person would need to do that. A serial killer? I don't think so. Why would he want to hide who he'd killed? He left the wallet of his last victim in the cage with him. He took Amos Thompson from the place he worked. No... no, only April Renee's identity was switched."

Ella was speaking quickly, frowning as she did, trying to piece it all together. "Because April needed to disappear. She needed to hide."

"Wh-what are you talking about?"

"You tell me, Ms. Renee. What did my dad have on you?"

The woman froze, swallowing. Her tongue darted out, testing her lips.

The coast guards had gone silent behind Ella now. They were like sentries at her back.

GEORGIA WAGNER

She kept glancing towards where their shadows cast by the moon flickered against the cold floor, fearful that one of them might lunge at her any moment.

One of the killers was a cop...

That's what April had said.

Was it true?

Was any of it?

Ella continued, slowly, marching forward, determined. Her hand never wavered, and she kept her gun aimed.

She knew that all sorts of things could be hidden in pretty packages.

Beauty was just as much camouflage as anything else.

And now she could see the cold in April Renee's eyes.

"This performance," Ella continued, slowly still, building up as the wind rose around them and the boat rocked, "It doesn't match a woman who'd steal from her boss's safe. Who'd then steal from a bank vault. Why was the safe here on the ship? With the notebook, with the flash drive..."

"What are you talking about!" April protested. But her voice wasn't quavering nearly as much now.

"You know exactly what I'm saying," Ella snapped, her voice severe now. "You killed at least four people. Maybe more. Why? What were

248

you trying to hide? Huh? What did my dad find out about you." Ella reached into her pocket now, with her offhand, and raised the small, leatherbound journal she'd taken from the safe. She waved it back and forth like a piece of meat in front of a hound's muzzle.

"Why?" Ella repeated, more firmly. "Hmm? You went to all this trouble to get this. You faked your own death. You killed multiple people..." And then her eyes widened. "Of course," she said. "Not just anyone... Amos Thompson was a criminal. He worked with organized crime. The man Brenner was hunting was a convict, escaped from prison... You were killing criminals..."

April Renee raised her one hand, placating. Her lip trembling. "I-I don't know what you're talking about. Please... please don't shoot me. Oh, God. He might still be on the ship!"

"Cut it out. I know you're lying!"

"I'm not!"

"It's the only thing that fits, April. My dad had something on you. Something horrible for you to go to all this trouble. What was it? What did you do?"

April just froze, staring at Ella, breathing slowly, her eyes flashing.

Ella needed to coax the bear from its cave. To reveal what really lurked beneath the surface.

Exposure.

The woman had faked her own death. Had stolen, had killed.

All of it to hide something.

The videos... a creepy person in shadow narrating. The digital clock taunting the cops.

The final two victims...

Priscilla Porter and Matthias Baker.

How did it all tie together?

"Revenge against my dad..." Ella said suddenly. "You wanted to kill Cilla and Mattie to get back at my father for blackmailing you."

The woman's eyes flashed again.

"That's it... isn't it?"

"I don't... don't know..."

"Just stop. Stop pretending. Here... why don't I see what it was you were hiding. Renee, right? I think it's alphabetical." Ella opened the leatherbound journal now.

She tensed as she did, her body poised.

And as she opened it, April began to breathe a bit more quickly, her eyes widened in horror. Fear.

Fear that was even deeper than the fear of a gun.

The fear of vanity.

The fear of someone whose entire life had been built on the perception of others.

Beauty was a gift...

Until it wasn't.

Ella knew it was true. Just like gold. Beauty made a great first impression... but the burden of maintaining that impression could be crippling. Beauty got gifts, favors, promotions...

It also received jealousy, envy, hatred... contempt.

Beautiful people, like April, could be tricked into thinking their beauty made them better than others.

The whole world screamed it at them.

Showed favors, held doors, reserved tables, asked on dates... The world taught them to value their looks over anything else.

And it was a trap.

It was fool's gold.

Vanity was a powerful motivator.

Ella opened the small leatherbound journal, flipping with one thumb and a forefinger, her gun still raised in her other hand.

The pages fluttered, caught by the wind, making sounds like the flapping wings of a bird.

And then Ella reached the last names that began with "R."

She scanned down the list.

Her father had dirt on so very many people, it was astounding.

Rogers. Infidelity.

Ramos. Murder. Bodies in gulley creek.

Raina. Fetishes.

And then... there...

Renee.

Ella stared at the entry next to Renee, April.

The Collective.

Ella stared at the entry. It didn't compute. *The Collective?* What did that mean?

Her eyes darted back up, searching April's face. The woman's expression had gone through something of a slow transformation.

Now, instead of a look of panic, she wore a scowl. Her expression had shifted like a ghoulish mask, moving from timid beauty to fierce severity.

Her eyes were narrowed, her brow lowered. The blood streaking the injury along her forehead tinged her eyebrow, staining it.

The woman let out a little breath, and then she whispered, "If you know all of this, then you know you should just let me go."

Even her voice seemed to switch.

Ella kept her gun raised, pointed at the woman. April's voice was now like steel. Cold and resolute and serpentine. There was even a sibilant hiss to her words as if she simply couldn't wait to utter the scathing language.

Ella stared at the woman. "What's the Collective?" she said simply, holding up the journal.

The woman shook her head. "You shouldn't have said that. You shouldn't have looked. Now, they're going to kill you."

"Who is?" Ella said, her skin prickling.

The woman's ghoulish expression still fixated on Ella, her eyes wide. The dark skies continued to lumber in, thick clouds swishing across the horizon. Spray from the ocean flecked over the vessel's railing, speckling Ella's neck and dappling her exposed skin along her arms and wrists.

Her hands remained steady, though, her feet set in a shooter's posture.

She slowly lowered the leather journal, slipping it back into her jacket pocket along with the flash drive.

All the other blackmail-referenced behaviors or crimes Ella knew. But this one... The Collective?

She felt a strange chill along her back.

For some reason, her mind shifted to Mortimer Graves, the serial murderer known as the Graveyard Killer. He'd also had an air of mystery around him.

But a dark, cloying, tombstone mystery. The type of secret that if left too long would fester and grow and decay.

"What is it?" Ella said, tapping her pocket. "The Collective? Is it a company? A job? A gang?"

April had twisted her face into a sneer now. "You don't know what you've done," she whispered.

"You sent those videos!" Ella retorted. "You said it was a game. You said it started in love! Why go to all the trouble? Why kill them?"

"It is a game!" April exclaimed, her eyes wide, her lips now peeling back into a jack-o-lantern leer. "And we drew first blood. We are on the leaderboard. Others will come. Others play too."

"What game?" Ella demanded. "Tell me?"

"There are only three rules," said April softly. "Only three..." Her eyes had gone cold. She slowly reached towards her waist.

"Don't you dare!" Ella said. "Don't do it!"

But the woman didn't move quickly. Instead, she spread her hands slowly, pulling the gun from her hip by the barrel, avoiding the trigger.

The two coast guards behind Ella were shouting warnings.

"Drop it!" Ella was yelling. She didn't want to fire. As much as her training would kick in, Ella had never been one to pull the trigger prematurely.

She had her own baggage when it came to flouting the rules.

She'd let the Graveyard Killer escape on purpose, hadn't she?

And so she kept her finger tense on the trigger but didn't shoot.

April's eyes, wide and leery were cranked to ten. Her skin around her lips had peeled back from her teeth, revealing the whites.

Slowly, she lowered her gun to the deck. *Clack.*

It lay there. She stepped over it and began moving, slowly, like a zombie walking.

"There's only three rules," she murmured to herself.

"Hey! Stop it! Hands up. Don't move!" Ella yelled.

But April didn't listen. She seemed almost to be in a trance. She was whispering to herself now. "Only three rules," she kept saying. Another step, past her gun on the deck, towards the railing of the ship.

"Stop! Stop now!"

But Ella's shouts fell on deaf ears.

The woman continued to approach, one step at a time, exhaling deeply, but the sound was carried away by the screeching wind, the creaking metal, the slosh of salt water.

She reached the rail, clasping her hands on the metal, her knuckles whitening where they gripped tightly.

April slowly turned her head, her eyes still wide, her lips still peeled back into a sneer.

"Only three rules," she whispered. "And we always, always, always play the game."

And with that, she threw her body over the side of the ship, into the raging sea below.

Ella lurched forward, her hand grazing April's foot.

But too late.

Ella stood gasping at the edge of the ship, staring over the rail, and she watched, dumbfounded. The woman's body hit the water with a splash, and then she was gone.

Leaning against the rail, Ella peered down into the dark water below. But there was nothing. No sign of the woman at all.

Only the churning of white froth, the steady spreading of ripples.

The coast guard were already moving, hastening down the side of the large ship, hand over hand, moving down the metal rungs.

Ella was hyperventilating where she stood, her breath coming rapidly.

There was nothing she could do.

For a tense moment, she considered it. Shot a glance at Hannah, making sure the woman was alright.

And then something came over Ella.

The reckless abandon that came with a spurt of adrenaline.

Stubborn with a smile according to some.

But to Ella...

She considered herself a bloodhound.

Once she caught the scent of a killer... she didn't stop. She never stopped.

And now, her teeth set, she shouted, "Bring the boat alongside!"

And then she leapt over the rail as well, refusing to allow April to get away.

Not even to escape into the hands of death.

Ella scythed through the air, cutting through high winds, and then, with a loud splash, she hit the water.

Chapter 25

The wet pounded against her body as she cut into it. Salt stung at her eyes and mouth. Everything was suddenly freezing cold and weighty around her as the ocean snared her.

She thrashed, churning bubbles, desperately trying to peer in the dark, dark water.

Her eyes stung as she struggled to keep them open, her lips sealed tight, holding onto her precious reserves of oxygen.

She trod water, trying to keep her body's natural buoyancy from carrying her back up. Her legs kicked under her, in the murk, steadying herself.

Her gaze scanned the depths, desperate and searching.

And then she saw it. A pale shape, barely visible in the dark.

It was a hand, reaching out from the depths.

Ella swam towards it, her arms slicing through the water, her heart pounding.

The hand was attached to a body, the body belonging to April.

The beautiful woman was still alive, but barely.

The cold water had smashed the life from her, the icy current threatening to take her under. She hung limp, suspended in the murk, slowly drifting down... the air having depleted from her lungs.

Likely intentionally.

A strange, stray thought—even in the cold—occurred to Ella. This woman had tried to kill herself.

But why?

Ella shivered, moving fast, her body kicking through the depths of the ocean...

The ocean.

The dreadful, horrible ocean.

And then memories flitted back. Her vision flickered, her mind rebelling against the water, the salt, the oppressive press of infinite weight.

Fear flooded her system.

Starting as a prickle, matching the cold around her, but then spreading into her heart like needles of ice.

She wanted to breathe but couldn't.

Bubbles escaped past her lips.

Fear and all its friends surged towards her, holding her in their grasp.

She'd always dreaded the ocean.

Priscilla often wore seashell earrings just to remind Ella of it.

Ella tried to calm herself as she swam, her eyes fixated on that single, pale, floating hand.

April was still drifting, slowly, careening towards the depths.

Ella swam harder, faster, her arms and legs aching, her lungs screaming for air.

Finally, with a mighty effort, she reached her, clasping her hand around April's wrist. Ella kicked faster, her limbs burning with effort.

She reached out with her other hand, her body shaking, and grabbed April's arm further up, clinging on tightly.

Ella struggled to force aside her fear. But bubbles fled her lips, carried away as she tried to push back towards the surface. She swam, feeling the woman's body grow heavier in her arms, her breath labored and weak.

And then April's eyes opened wide, staring like two moons.

Ella's heart leapt. April let out a scream—or at least contorted her face into the appearance of one. Her mouth open, her eyes wide, her eyebrows skyrocketing up towards the gash on her head where a thin, gossamer strand of blood flitted in the sea.

Terror.

Abject terror in April's eyes.

Not scared of Ella—not in the least.

But of something Ella represented. Something deeper still.

Ella didn't know how to react at first, trying to hold on tight.

And then April began to thrash and kick.

Instead of escaping towards the surface of the ocean, though, she tried to cut *down* towards the darker sections of the water.

Ella still tried to hang on, but April was whipping, kicking, trying to drown herself, cutting with weakened motions *down* into the darkness.

Something had this woman so scared, so frightened, that she would rather drown herself than face it.

The Collective.

What was it?

Thoughts pelted around Ella's mind like the bubbles scraping past her cheeks.

How was her father involved?

And why had April been willing to kill to keep it quiet? Why go through the farce of pretending to be some serial killer—was that what it had been? A pretense.

Two of the victims had criminal connections—three if they included the escaped convict's girlfriend. Two were unidentified. Another, Hannah Bartlow, had escaped.

Ella cut in the water, her lungs aching, darting down.

Now, April didn't just represent a killer.

But a piece of the puzzle.

Someone who was the linchpin to all of this.

Perhaps, even, someone who could get her father put behind bars.

Ella kicked, her mind screaming now, along with her lungs. Panic and fear protested her efforts, but she didn't slow.

She tried to snag at April's leg again. Now, they were at least twenty feet below the surface.

April was still trying to descend.

The oppressive weight of the ocean around them crushed down on them.

But Ella didn't give up.

Stubborn.

This time she wasn't smiling.

Her features were strained, her heart in her throat, her legs above her head, kicking desperately, like a single beam of light in an infinite black night, she cut through the ocean, the source of her childhood fear.

But fear had never controlled Ella Porter.

She'd left a family of comfort and wealth. Had worked with a serial killer in order to accomplish an impossible goal.

She wasn't what others thought she was.

Her will was something of iron.

Like Cilla.

Ella kicked faster, scowling now, thinking of her sister's seashell earrings.

She tried to snag April's foot again.

But this time received a kick for her efforts. Pain exploded across her lips, but she recovered quick enough. Still, another burst of bubbles had exploded from her mouth.

Her oxygen was rapidly running out.

But she didn't give up.

She forced herself to move faster, her arms and legs pleading for her to stop, her lungs burning with the demand for air.

But Ella's mind focused determinedly on the task ahead.

She reached out, her hand finding April's leg, and with a mighty effort, she grabbed a third time.

April screamed silently, but this time no bubbles escaped. She had no air left to give. Her eyes widened as she tried to fight Ella off, her body jerking and fighting, but Ella didn't let go.

With a burst of effort, she pulled the woman towards the surface.

April fought the entire way, but eventually, April's motions slowed. Her head lolled.

Ella had managed to outlast the woman, barely clinging to consciousness.

Ella kicked again… again.

Which direction was up?

Her arm was now wrapped around the killer's chest. Where was up? Up?

Her panic reached a crescendo.

Another kick.

Another.

A—

Relief as the two of them breached the surface.

She spotted the slick hull of the cutter yards away, churning water and riding the rolling ocean. Up and down, hills of water carried Ella and her quarry.

Ella tugged insistently. She kept swimming, breathing greedily, exhaling in pants until finally she reached the Coast Guard boat, and with their help, pulled April up and out of the cold water.

The woman was alive but unconscious.

Ella had saved a killer's life.

Again.

The coast guards began to move quickly, getting an oxygen mask over April's face and wrapping her in a blanket where she lay on the deck, barely breathing.

Ella stood there panting, her heart pounding, her mind spinning.

She had to know.

What was the game?

What were the rules?

What was the Collective?

What the hell had all of this been, and how was her father involved?

The coast guards seemed to sense her urgency, and they moved quickly to get April onto a cushioned seat to help her come to once more.

Ella followed them, her mind a whirlwind as she tried to make sense of it all.

She scowled at the back of April's head as the Coast Guard carted her away.

The cutter moved back to the side of the ship in order to recover Hannah as well.

Ella scowled, reaching for her cuffs and approaching where April lay.

"Playing possum won't work a third time," she muttered.

But April didn't move, the beautiful woman's head lolled to the side where she was set in a cushioned chair.

She was breathing still.

One of the officers began checking her vitals.

Ella let out a long, silent breath.

They'd caught the killer.

And, with some trepidation, she wondered how things were going on Brenner's side of the equation.

Chapter 26

Ella stared through the glass of the ICU room, strangely numb.

In one bed, her sister lay with an arm wrapped in a sling. "She was shot," a doctor said at her side. "He got to her just in time. Brought her in with a rock truck." The doctor shook his head, a neatly trimmed beard swishing. "Never seen anything like it."

Ella just stared at the bed with her sister, that same numb feeling spreading.

Her eyes then moved towards the second bed in the hospital room, separated only by a thin curtain.

Brenner Gunn lay there, his chest bandaged in white, his eyes closed. A heartbeat monitor flashed at the side of the bed across a green, backlit screen. He looked so peaceful lying there.

"And what about him?" she murmured.

"Shot," said the well-groomed doctor reflexively. His voice sounded weary.

He'd been with the two gunshot victims for nearly three hours before Ella had been allowed upstairs.

When she'd heard the news over the radio, after returning to the docks, she'd handed April Renee and Hannah Bartlow off to the Coast Guard, then drove straight to the hospital.

She hadn't been able to *sit* in the waiting room but had paced.

And now, she felt as if the blood was leaving her face. Her skin prickled as she tapped a foot against the tiled ground.

The doctor was shaking his head. "It doesn't look good," he said.

Ella stared at him. "Don't say that."

The doctor just shrugged, rubbing at the bridge of his nose and releasing a weary sigh.

The doctor said, "Well, I agreed to show you them, but you need to leave now. It's going to be touch-and-go for the next few weeks." Ella shot a quick look at the doctor.

"I need to speak to them," she said.

"He's unconscious."

"She's not," Ella cut in, pointing at her sister. Normally, Ella wasn't the type to be so blunt, but now she found she didn't really care.

She jabbed a finger once more through the glass, insistently. "I need to speak with my sister."

The doctor glanced at the twin, then back at Ella. He said, "She's coming in and out of consciousness. The amount of pain meds she's on will leave her incoherent. She won't know what she's saying."

Ella shook her head. "I still need to speak with her."

"You can't. You agreed to see them and leave, Agent Porter. Now, please."

He tried to put his hand against her back to guide her away, but she stiffened, glaring at him.

He pushed a bit more insistently.

"Please," he repeated, a bit more forcefully, giving another little push. "Don't make me call security."

For a moment, Ella thought about digging her heels in, about demanding her way. It was what Priscilla would've done.

But Ella and Priscilla had never been similar.

Ella didn't believe that courage had to look like rage. Nor did it have to be Brenner's version of a direct, headlong approach.

No... She had her own tactics.

And so she shrugged, stumbling into him, her hand sliding across his chest.

He grunted from the force of her motion, and she apologized.

At the same time, she palmed the magnetic ID card he'd shown her on the way in, clipped inside his pocket.

Then, card in hand, she allowed the attending physician to guide her down a cold, marble hall lined with fake plants and exuding the tinge of ammonia.

He led her out into a waiting lobby, double-checked the doors were locked behind him for the intensive care unit, and then gave her a long look, adjusting his white jacket.

"I mean it," he said. "You need to leave."

She forced a quick nod. "Just let me process," she said. "I'll head out in a bit."

He sighed, gestured at one of the chairs next to a wooden table covered in magazines, and then, once she'd seated herself, he gave her another suspicious glance. He opened his mouth for some final comment, but then he touched his hand to a pager that suddenly started vibrating on his hip.

He cursed, turned on his heel, and hastened down the steps, leaving her alone outside the locked door.

She waited for his shadow to disappear, trying to look hunched and defeated.

But once he was gone, the sound of his footsteps receding, the scent of ammonia going with him, she regained her feet with surefooted steps, marched right back to the door, swiped her stolen keycard, watched the light turn green, then slipped into the hall on the other side.

She moved hurriedly, her footsteps tapping on the linoleum floor and past closed doors that seemed to go on forever.

Finally, she reached her sister's room and peered in through the glass.

The sight of her twin stirred a wave of emotion in her chest.

Ella felt a spark of anger and a twinge of sorrow as she saw her sister's injuries. Her eyes moved to Brenner's as well. A new spark of grief—stronger than the first.

He'd kissed her back on that ship.

And she'd withdrawn.

She'd pretended as if it hadn't happened.

A lance of regret sparked through her. Guilt followed closely behind. She'd been the one who sent him back to check on Cilla. She'd thought he'd be safe.

But according to the report, he'd shot four men.

Another reason she'd flouted the doctor's orders.

Four gunmen had hunted down Cilla and Brenner.

Four gunmen working with April Renee.

Not a serial killer.

Something else.

The Collective—whatever that meant.

She scowled, staring down at her sister's form once more. Brenner's heartbeat monitor continued to flash, and she kept glancing at it, distracted, as if double-checking he was still alive.

Part of her wanted to go over to him, hold his hand and just stand there.

But she swallowed this impulse, cursing inwardly that she couldn't.

Brenner wasn't conscious.

And it wouldn't help anyone if she passed up this opportunity.

Her sister, on the other hand, was awake. Coming in and out of consciousness, as the doctor had said, juiced up on pain meds.

Which was why Ella had returned.

It was a painful thing, and it tore at her to look away from Brenner. She could have watched him for hours. But now, she consciously turned her back on him, forcing the image from her mind.

Something else was afoot.

Something that involved Jameson Porter's safety deposit box. A journal full of blackmail targets, and a USB drive with evidence for the blackmail.

And all of it came back to April Renee and Officer Taylor—the cop, according to the coroner, who'd gone rogue and shot Brenner.

The three *other* gunmen had criminal connections. The same as Amos Thompson and the escaped convict who'd been found in the crab pot to start all of this.

Was April involved in organized crime?

Then why send the taunting videos?

Why play those games on the boat with the knife? She'd already seen the cuts on April Renee's arm. The woman had pretended to be a man, scrambling her voice, using a knife to inflict pain on herself.

Hannah Bartlow had looked terrified. Why go to all the trouble?

It still didn't make sense.

It didn't click into place.

April and Officer Taylor were the killers. That much was clear. But more was going on here.

It was as if...

As if organized crime had *hired* serial killers for something.

Ella wrinkled her nose.

That seemed to fit *almost*. But not quite. She was still missing something.

Which was why she was now standing next to her sister's bed.

She stayed with her sister for a long while, not saying a word, just watching her breathe until, finally, Cilla's eyelids fluttered again, and she seemed to rouse once more.

Ella smiled down at her sister, trying to make the expression disarming.

Cilla was still wearing seashell earrings.

Ella's expression flickered, but she kept the smile in place.

Lying with your expression... Brenner often accused her of this.

She decided perhaps he was right.

Another lance of guilt and regret, but she shoved these emotions aside, refusing to look back at Brenner.

"Ella?" whispered Cilla, staring at her sister through bleary eyes.

This was why Ella had come.

On pain meds, injured, half-conscious, Cilla's guard would be down.

Ella bit her lip, drawing blood. The pain felt like penance. She didn't feel proud of what she was about to do.

Questioning a woman who hated her while she was vulnerable...

But Jameson Porter was involved.

The journal that had sparked April's murder spree had been his.

And Cilla was in charge of his inland mining company. If anyone knew what was going on, what had caused all of this, it would be her sister.

"Cilla," Ella said softly, keeping her voice calm.

"Hmm?" a low moan, another flutter. It looked as if Cilla had fallen asleep again.

Ella bit her lip, waiting. She glanced up nervously, looking through the glass, but the door to the ICU was still closed.

"Cilla," she said more urgently.

"Hmm?"

"How are you?"

"Bad..." Cilla whispered. "What... what's... where am I?"

It pained Ella to see her sister like this. Cilla, for all her flaws, had always been strong. With a spine of steel.

Now, though, she looked exhausted. Tired. Bandaged. Her face was scraped up.

"How's Mattie?" Cilla whispered.

"Alive. Well. He only was knocked unconscious from the fall. He's fine. He's worried about you."

Cilla snickered. Though it was more like the giggle of a young child. Her eyes fluttered again, but her lips turned into a smile.

Ella was stunned.

It wasn't a sneer or a smirk but, rather, a good-natured, pleased smile.

The sort of smile Ella hadn't seen on her sister's face for many years.

As quickly as the smile had come, though, it faded. "He always worries," whispered Cilla in a hoarse voice. She paused. "Ella?" she said again, and she started to frown.

Ella guessed that Cilla was starting to remember the animosity between them. One of them choosing their family, the gold, the kingdom of the Porters.

The other leaving, joining the FBI.

Neither of them really understood the other.

Ella wasn't here to mend fences though. It pained her. It made her stomach hurt, but she was here to get information.

"Cilla," she said, biting her tongue in between so she wouldn't sob at the deception. She pushed aside the emotion again. "I need to know..." She paused, wondering how to phrase it.

"Ella?" Cilla said, recognition starting to spark. The frown was deepening. The heartbeat monitor rising.

So Ella didn't wait. She just spat out the question. "What's the Collective? How's dad involved?"

Cilla blinked once. Snickered this time. She seemed to relax briefly. "The Collective? Nothing. Made up."

"What is it?"

"Nothing."

"It's not nothing."

"It's just a lie. Something people pretend."

"What do you mean? Pretend it's what?"

"Real."

Ella could feel her frustration mounting. "Real in what way?"

Cilla just shrugged. "I don't know. I just know it scares people. Really, really badly."

"You know more than that!" Ella protested. "You have to."

"No... No, I don't."

Ella sighed in frustration.

"I mean... if it was real..." Cilla snorted, shaking her head. "No... No, it's not though."

"What is it?" Ella demanded.

"If it was real?" Cilla asked, confused.

"Yeah. Yeah, pretend it was real. What is it?"

Cilla paused...

And then the strangest change occurred. Her face suddenly went pale, her lips white. Terror flashed in her eyes. Her heartbeat spiked, and she began hyperventilating, shaking her head and moaning as she did.

"What is it?" Ella said. "Are you okay?"

She suddenly spotted movement at the end of the hall. The ICU door was opening. A man in a white coat was glaring, marching towards her, stroking his impressive beard.

Ella looked away from where he was waving angrily at her.

She looked back at her sister.

"What is The Collective? Please? Why did April kill all of those people?"

"Ask her!" Cilla said, her voice a moan, her eyes not quite seeing, struggling under the blankets on the bed. But then, she let out a long breath, and even in her pained, drugged state, Ella could see her sister exerting willpower.

A spine of steel.

Cilla calmed, her heartbeat still racing, but her expression didn't show it.

For a brief moment, she met Ella's gaze. And it was almost as if she were lucid. She stared... swallowed, then said, "A game... A game that *they* play. Only one winner."

"What sort of game? Who's *they*?"

"Murderers. Degenerates. People with absolutely no regard for human life." Cilla let out a long breath. "Truly, truly sick twists."

"I don't understand. It's a game serial killers play?"

"Mhmm."

"Ms. Porter!" snapped a voice in the doorway.

The doctor had arrived.

And this time, he hadn't come alone. Ella winced, glancing past him and spotting two burly security guards moving behind the doctor, huffing as they hastened down the hall.

Ella looked back at Priscilla.

"And April Renee? How was she involved?"

"Huh? Oh... Renee?" A faint flicker of recognition. Then a nod. "I see... She was always crazy."

"How was she involved! What about Officer Taylor?"

A snort of derision. "Taylor was always April's bitch. She never loved him. But he loved her. Why? What did they do?"

Everyone in Nome knew each other if they stuck around long enough. Cilla was in the business of knowing.

Did she have access to the same blackmail her father did?

But now, the coherence was fading again. Cilla didn't quite recognize her sister, it seemed.

Or at least had forgotten how much they didn't get along.

Now, though, the security guards had reached Ella.

She held up her hands apologetically. "Fine! Fine, I'm going!"

They grabbed at her arm, and Cilla glanced at where her sister was being manhandled.

Ella didn't yank her arm away though. Cilla smirked, and Ella looked straight ahead, marching back out of the ICU.

The doctor tried to lecture her, but Ella wasn't in the mood to hear it.

She shot a final glance back towards Brenner, double-checking he was still breathing.

Something about seeing his heartbeat on the monitor filled her with a flicker of hope.

She breathed a bit easier as she apologized, being escorted down the hall by the two security guards while the doctor remained behind, checking on his patients.

Cilla's words haunted Ella as she moved away.

A game played by killers?

What sort of game?

What had Ella just stumbled on?

At least there was a connection between Taylor and Renee. Some sort of unrequited love. A woman with Renee's beauty wouldn't have had much trouble getting a man like Taylor to do her bidding.

The three gunmen, though? Criminals.

At least three of the victims? Associated with criminals...

It didn't make sense.

Not completely.

And Ella realized, as she was jostled down the stairs, that it likely wouldn't.

Not yet.

The Collective...

She didn't know what it was.

Her father was somehow involved, which meant he was going to hide everything he could. He would keep her in the dark.

As she moved down the banister, taking the next flight of stairs, leaving the ICU and the haunting beep and buzz of machines behind her, her eyes narrowed.

She tugged her arm free of the security guard with a practiced jerking motion, and skipped two stairs ahead, moving towards lobby doors.

She didn't look back, ignoring their protests. Her phone buzzed. She glanced down and cursed. Maddie had texted. Ella had completely forgotten about her promise of meeting up with her younger cousin.

Ella sighed, vowing to reschedule as soon as she could.

She pocketed her phone again, still keeping ahead of her burly escort.

When one of them tried to catch up with her, she flashed her badge, her eyes as cold as ice.

He withdrew his hand.

She turned and stepped through the sliding doors, past a bench and another fake plant.

The scent of stale bagels caught her nose, and the crisp, clean Nome air fell across her face.

In the distance, she spotted the water, facing the hospital, waves lapping against the shore.

The sea still scared her.

But it wouldn't stop her.

Her father wouldn't either.

He was involved in all of this. She'd caught the killer. Solved the case.

But there was more to this one.

She could feel it in her bones.

And she wasn't going to stop digging until she found out what.

Other Books by Georgia Wagner

Artemis Blythe Series

The skeletons in her closet are twitching...

Genius chessmaster and FBI consultant Artemis Blythe swore she'd
never return to the misty Cascade Mountains.

Her father—a notorious serial killer, responsible for the deaths of seven women—is now imprisoned, in no small part due to a clue she provided nearly fifteen years ago.

And now her father wants his vengeance.

A new serial killer is hunting the wealthy and the elite in the town of Pinelake. Artemis' father claims he knows the identity of the killer, but he'll only tell daughter dearest. Against her will, she finds herself forced back to her old stomping grounds.

Once known as a child chess prodigy, now the locals only think of her as 'The Ghostkiller's' daughter.In the face of a shamed family name and a brother involved with the Seattle mob, Artemis endeavors to use her tactical genius to solve the baffling case.

Hunting a murderer who strikes without a trace, if she fails, the next skeleton in her closet will be her own.

Other Books by Georgia Wagner

Sophie Quinn Series

A cold knife, a brutal laugh. Then the odds-defying escape.

Once a hypnotist with her own TV show, now, Sophie Quinn works as a full-time consultant for the FBI. Everything changed six years ago. She can still remember that horrible night. Slated to be the River

Killer's tenth victim, she managed to slip her bindings and barely escape where so many others failed. Her sister wasn't so lucky.

And now the killer is back.

Two PHDs later, she's now a rising star at the FBI. Her photographic memory helps solve crimes, but also helps her to never forget. She saw the River Killer's tattoo. She knows what he sounds like. And now, ten years later, he's active again.

Sophie Quinn heads back home to the swamps of Louisiana, along the Mississippi River, intent on evening the score and finding the man who killed her sister. It's been six years since she's been home, though. Broken relationships and shattered dreams exist among the bayous, the rivers, the waterways and swamps of Louisiana; can Sophie find her way home again? Or will she be the River Killer's next victim to float downstream?

Want to know more?

Greenfield press is the brainchild of bestselling author Steve Higgs. He specializes in writing fast paced adventurous mystery and urban fantasy with a humorous lilt. Having made his money publishing his own work, Steve went looking for a few 'special' authors whose work he believed in.

Georgia Wagner was the first of those, but to find out more and to be the first to hear about new releases and what is coming next, you can join the Facebook group by copying the following link into your browser - www.facebook.com/GreenfieldPress

About the Author

Georgia Wagner worked as a ghost writer for many, many years before finally taking the plunge into self-publishing. Location and character are two big factors for Georgia, and getting those right allows the story to flow seamlessly onto the page. And flow it does, because Georgia is so prolific a new term is required to describe the rate at which nerve-tingling stories find their way into print.

When not found attached to a laptop, Georgia likes spending time in local arboretums, among the trees and ponds. An avid cultivator of orchids, begonias, and all things floral, Georgia also has a strong penchant for art, paintings, and sculptures. A many-decades long passion for mystery novels and years of chess tournament experience makes Georgia the perfect person to pen the Artemis Blythe series.

Printed in Great Britain
by Amazon